Also by Saïd Sayrafiezadeh

WHEN SKATEBOARDS WILL BE FREE: A MEMOIR

Brief Encounters
with the Enemy

Brief Encounters with the Enemy

FICTION

Saïd Sayrafiezadeh

THE DIAL PRESS NEW YORK

Copyright © 2013 by Saïd Sayrafiezadeh

Published in the United States by The Dial Press, an imprint of
The Random House Publishing Group,
a division of Random House, Inc., New York.

DIAL PRESS and the HOUSE colophon are registered trademarks of
Random House, Inc.

"Cartography" originally appeared in *The Paris Review* in slightly
different form as "Most Livable City." "Appetite," "Paranoia," and "A
Brief Encounter With the Enemy" originally appeared in *The New Yorker*.

Library of Congress Cataloging-in-Publication Data
Sayrafiezadeh, Saïd.
Brief encounters with the enemy : fiction / Saïd Sayrafiezadeh.
pages cm
ISBN 978-0-8129-9358-5
eBook ISBN 978-0-8129-9359-2
I. Title.
PS3619.A998B75 2013
813'.6—dc23   2013019916

Printed in the United States of America on acid-free paper

www.dialpress.com

2   4   6   8   9   7   5   3   1

First Edition

Book design by Liz Cosgrove

For Karen Mainenti and Steven Kuchuck

Contents

Brief Encounters
with the Enemy

CARTOGRAPHY

The winter the bus drivers went on strike I was twenty-three years old and living on the edge of the city in a neighborhood that was on the verge of becoming a ghetto. The parks had closed, and so had the supermarket, and also the elementary school, and every night the streetlights appeared to have gotten dimmer. The easiest way into and out of the neighborhood was by crossing through an underpass, but everyone had stopped using that. Instead, we took the long way up the hill and over the thoroughfare that ran six lanes. It was no longer a surprise to pick up the morning newspaper and learn that there had been yet another regrettable occurrence in the neighborhood the previous day. In the middle of the night, I would be jolted out of my dreams sometimes by the sound of police sirens or fire engines or car alarms or once even the voice of a man, just beneath my bedroom window, cooing submissively, "Please take my wallet."

Earlier that fall, things had taken a turn for the worse when I had been fired from a good job as a cartographer in a design studio that I had worked in for only about four months. The owner of the firm was a tubby, bearded, gregarious, well-read man named Ned Frost, who had large white teeth and a habit of vigorously rubbing his hands together when he laughed, as if he were attempting to start a fire with his palms. He wore tweed jackets, had bad breath, and fancied himself a poet. "I am the state's leading poet," he had announced once to everyone in the office—this despite having never been published. When I had first met him, he seemed pleasant, unassuming, charming even, and on my third day of work he had taken me out to a special lunch, and then a few days later out to a special dinner to discuss "the work that lies ahead." He seemed to find many of the things I said delightful, and a few times he leaned back in his chair and laughed and rubbed his hands together. His interest in me gave me confidence that I was someone who might have a bright future after all. But no more than three weeks after I had started working for him, he informed me that I was a closeted gay man and that if only I had the courage to admit this, then the two of us could be together. During the day, instead of doing work, he would compose long, meandering letters to me that began with "My Dearest Rex" and included phrases such as "and yes, yes, I saw you standing there, yes" or "there is a leaning into warmth, a leaningintoness that only eyes know." I could hear him typing away in the adjacent office, and I would know that the printer beside my desk would soon begin to hum and out would come five, six, seven single-spaced pages. An hour or so later, he would enter and stand by my desk, hovering, shifting from foot to foot, his hands deep in his pockets jingling coins, pretending to busy himself with files, waiting for me to initiate conversation.

I had learned from a female intern that I was just one in a succession of young men whom Ned Frost had hired, courted, and then, when they rebuffed him, fired. I wanted to keep the job, of course, so I tried my best to pretend things were normal and aboveboard. My only identifiable skill was apparently an ability—recognized by Ned Frost—to design maps, and I envisioned myself as a great failure if I allowed this once-in-a-lifetime opportunity at a vocation to slip away. "You have to walk through the doors when they've been opened for you," my father often counseled. Sometimes I would wonder if I was imagining Ned Frost's advances, if I was exaggerating the nature of his interest in me. "Perhaps I am overplaying all of this," I would reason with myself, and it would help me to feel calm and even hopeful. But one afternoon any ambiguity was finally put to rest when, at the end of an immense sixteen-page letter about the movie *E.T.*—particularly the scene in which the alien presses his throbbing finger against the young boy—Ned Frost signed off, "My cock feels full with the thought of you in my heart."

It was winter now and it was cold and the bus drivers were on strike. And the war was coming, everybody said so. Because of this confluence of events no one was sympathetic to the drivers' cause. It was seen as a selfish act of sabotage. Each night the mayor would make an appearance on the news, explaining how this wasn't the time for individuals to worry about personal gain. "Now is the time to come together," he'd say. In reality, it was only poor people who needed to ride the bus, so they were essentially the ones who were affected by the strike, scrambling to get to work by any means, sometimes eight to a car. The only poor person I knew who wasn't affected was my neighbor Frankie, a fifty-year-old man who lived across the hall from me and whose left side had been paralyzed by a stroke several years earlier. It took enormous effort for him to stand or walk, and he went outside on average twice a month, once to the bank and once to the post office. He also had a difficult time speaking, and when the news first broke of the strike, he stood in his doorway grinning at me and stammering, "I could care . . . I could care . . . less!" For him the strike had become a great equalizer, handicapping everyone, including me.

In spite of his miserable physical condition, Frankie was easygoing, affable, a man who had come to accept his lot in life. I believed I would have killed myself if I had to scrape down the stairwell like him, doing in five minutes what a two-year-old could do in thirty seconds, but he never complained. He had become adept at managing everything himself, mostly by using his right hand, and he would adamantly turn down any offers of assistance.

"I can help you with that, Frankie," I'd say, watching him wrestle with a can opener as if it were a live fish.

"Look at me! Look at me!" he'd exclaim proudly, and the can of beans would pop open.

A lifetime of alcoholism had been responsible for his

stroke, so he had only himself to blame. This seemed to be an empowering thought for him, and he repeated it often and with great intensity. "Me!" he'd say, and tap his chest. "Me!"

When I had first moved into the apartment and seen Frankie standing in the hallway in a dirty white T-shirt, leaning on his rocker, stubble and no teeth, I was frightened and repulsed. He struck me as a pervert, a degenerate, the kind of man who would have dressed in a trench coat. Then one evening he knocked on my door, handed me a few crumpled dollar bills, and asked if I would do him a big favor and buy him three boxes of M&M's. "Two . . . two . . . peanut. And one plain." I told him I was busy, sorry, and shut the door. Then I felt guilty, went out into the hallway to find him shuffling off in slow motion, took his money, walked six blocks to the Buy 'n' Save and bought him what he wanted. After that he began inviting me over to share the Chinese food he would order. "I can't . . . I can't . . . eat all this shit," he'd tell me. At first I took cynical advantage of his generosity, sitting on his couch, stuffing my face with chow mein, thinking the entire time that listening to him sputter on for half an hour wasn't a bad trade-off for a good meal. But after a while I began to enjoy his company, and I would look forward to him inviting me over so I could hear his stories about working as a low-level manager in a VA hospital. "I never did . . . a damn thing!" he'd say, and his shoulders would shake with laughter. Eventually I ceased to be nauseated by the fact that he ate with his fingers, kept his false teeth in a glass on the table, blew his nose into an old pair of underpants, and pissed into an aluminum cooking pot while standing in the living room because it was too difficult to walk to the bathroom. "Pardon me," he'd say, and unzip himself. After our meal was over, we would sit around and watch basketball on his cable. Frankie told me that he had been a star basketball player when he was in high school, a story I found hard to believe and which I kept making a point to look up but never did. "They all suck," he'd say of the players on television.

In the beginning the experts thought the strike would last only a few days, but after two weeks it was going strong with no end in sight. A neighbor took pity on me and drove me to the supermarket, where I bought enough food to feed a family of five, but other than that, I was unable to leave the neighborhood. I would walk around in the cold afternoons like a convict exiled to Siberia, ignored by the authorities because the region was too vast to flee. There was the empty playground, there was the Buy 'n' Save, there was the laundromat with the ever present attendant who sat motionless like a bear in a zoo. The wind would whip across the flat land. In the evening I would sit around waiting for Frankie to knock on my door and invite me over. On the rare occasions when he didn't, I would take out a zucchini and a carrot from the refrigerator, sauté them in a pan, and put them on top of a bed of pasta, then cover everything with an excessive amount of Parmesan cheese. As I ate, it was impossible for me to avoid reflecting on the possibility that the bus strike would never end, which led me to consider that the general condition of my life would also remain as it was.

The day after Ned Frost gave me the *E.T.* letter, I walked

into his office unannounced and said that I didn't want to receive any more letters like that or I would sue him for sexual harassment. It seemed like the right thing to say. From his desk he stared up at me sheepishly, silently. He looked like a balloon, as if someone had blown up a shirt and tie.

"There is a warmth I've felt toward you," he said poetically.

The prospect of being entrapped in a romantic exchange unnerved me. "I don't care about your warmth, Ned," I said.

"And there is a warmth," he continued as if I hadn't said a word, "yes, that I have felt *from* you."

I said nothing.

"Would you deny," he suddenly demanded, "that you have ever had a warm thought for me?" There was accusation in his voice. I looked back at him sternly. Then he burst into tears. "I've never felt as close to anyone as I do toward you," he managed to get out.

It was hard not to be moved by this, and I felt sorry for him and wondered if I was being needlessly cruel. But I had to remain resolute—for his own good. "Just consider yourself warned," I said.

The next day, as I was trying to map out a particularly complicated cloverleaf interchange, the printer beside me began to hum. This time it was only one page, and it contained a single line: "I cannot live one more day with hearts on edge." An hour later I was fired.

There were no basketball games on television, so Frankie and I sat around eating orange chicken while he regaled me with stories about an old girlfriend that he had been madly in love with but had failed to marry because he couldn't stop drinking.

"Black," he said. "She was . . . black." Then he paused. "I like brown skin." He shrugged. The matter was out of his control.

We channel-surfed for a while. I kept hoping he'd stop on the spring break swimsuit movie, but all he did when we came around to it was say, "Bullshit." We watched a bit of the local news coverage of the strike, in which the same three video clips were aired repeatedly: the transit chairman in a suit and tie, calmly laying out his side of the story, which seemed fair enough; a group of picketers dressed in hats and scarves and gloves, standing in an empty parking lot, chanting wildly as they waved their signs; and finally, a man-on-the-street interview with a soldier who'd just been called up and who said, looking directly into the camera, "I understand you want more money, but now isn't the time." The anchorman, who'd been delivering the news in the city for fifty years and looked near death, said that the day's negotiations had ended "acrimoniously."

"What's that mean?" I asked Frankie.

"What?"

" 'Acrimonious,' what's it mean?"

But he had landed on an old black-and-white foreign movie. "I know this!" he shouted. "I know this!"

I had never seen the film, and since it was half over and since it was foreign, I had no idea what was going on and didn't care enough to try to figure it out. I kept waiting for Frankie to switch over to something else, but he never did, so

I just sat there quietly while it played. When we got to the end, with the main character sobbing and crawling around drunkenly on his hands and knees, I snorted derisively and turned to Frankie, who was staring at the screen with tears in his eyes.

"He . . . he did it . . . to himself. To himself!"

Then, with all the energy he had, Frankie pushed himself to a standing position, unzipped his pants, and grabbed ahold of his pot. "Pardon me," he said.

On the twenty-eighth day of the strike, I decided I couldn't stand my confinement any longer. Early that morning I set off with a small bag of food to walk as far as I could. I crossed through the underpass quickly, without incident, and out of the neighborhood. The city, unfortunately, had not been designed for walking, and there would come times when I'd find myself trying to circumvent a freeway, or circling back from a dead-end street, or going for long stretches without a sidewalk. The air was chilly, but the sky was bright, and I could feel that spring was nearing. I kept the pace brisk and lively. But after about an hour, my energy began to wane. I pressed on, trying to ignore the nagging awareness that I would have to retrace every one of the steps I was now taking. I walked through parks and neighborhoods and shopping centers, many of which I had never seen or known existed. There were people out, but the city felt more vacant than usual. After the factories had closed, anybody who had the means picked up and moved away, leaving the city with empty smokestacks and the second oldest population in the country. What was I still doing here? I was too young to inhabit the ends of the earth.

Several cars passed me going the other way, and I considered sticking my thumb out and hitching a ride back home, but I wasn't sure if people did that anymore.

I walked along the boulevard that divided the east side of the city from the west side, and I passed the restaurant I had worked in as a short-order cook. It wasn't open yet for business, but the windows were already fogged with steam from the kitchen. An American flag hung in the front window next to a sign advertising half-price brick-oven pizza on Thursday nights. I remembered vividly the grueling twelve-hour shifts, the beer reward at the end of the night, the pretty waitresses, the black cooks who had gotten addicted to crack. If we wanted a meal, we had to pay for it, so I would surreptitiously cook myself food and then eat it while hiding in the bathroom stall, sitting on the toilet. At the time I thought that I had managed to even the playing field.

Two hours after I had begun my journey, I realized I was lost. I turned back the way I came, but the way I came could no longer be discerned. There were four streets curving and winding their way toward me. I chose one and followed it for ten minutes until I was certain it was the wrong one, and then I turned back around. But now I was faced with four more streets, each one looking identical and vaguely familiar. I passed through a wealthy, tree-lined neighborhood with curbside mailboxes into a neighborhood that was not so wealthy but still had trees. I walked along railroad tracks for a while. The sun was starting to drop and it was getting colder. My feet and legs ached and I wanted to sit, but to sit at a time like this felt irresponsible. Beside me were woods, and beyond them I could make out the river. This was the true boulevard of the city that for decades had brought coal in and taken goods out. The glory years. If I waited long enough, I'd probably see a gunship float past.

I came into a neighborhood that looked like it had been abandoned. The whole place was gray and rotting and lacking any trace of life. I sat down on the steps of a two-story brick house with an addition covered in aluminum siding, and the moment I did, a wiry woman appeared on the porch across the way and looked at me. She was wearing a nightgown that she clutched around her. An old man in pajamas came and stood at her side. I took out my lunch and ate it while I watched them confer.

"There ain't no one living in there now," the woman said.

"That's okay," I said.

They conferred again.

"Hey, mister."

"What?"

"There ain't no one in there now."

"I heard you the first time," I said.

They looked startled. The man took a step forward like he wouldn't stand for that kind of talk. I got up and stretched my legs. My feet felt swollen. I moved on.

"Hey, mister," the woman said as I passed. "Is the strike still on?"

"No," I said, "it's over."

"What'd he say?"

"Hey, mister," the man called, "when's the strike going to be over?"

* * *

It was dusk, and I didn't know what to do. I turned left and then left again. Was I going in a circle? I thought about how the cooks would be starting their shift at the restaurant. A car pulled up beside me. "Would you like a ride?" a friendly voice asked. I looked in the window and saw Ned Frost's bearded face smiling up at me. "Were you going to walk the whole way?" he asked. Then incredulously: "You weren't going to *walk the whole way*!"

There was a young man about my age sitting in the passenger seat.

"I was," I said.

Ned guffawed. "Young legs." Was there subtext in that? "We're heading your way," he said, "and we've got two empty seats."

The young man got out to let me in the back. He glanced at me with a mixture of shell shock and glumness. He was tall and thin with a tie that he'd tied too short. He had razor nicks on his neck. "Nice to meet you," he mumbled.

Ned sped off. I marveled at the amount of distance a car could cover in such a short time. In two minutes I was back in familiar territory. I listened to the conversation going on in the front seat, but whatever was being discussed was sparse and hushed. I thought about telling Ned that he could let me out, that I could make it the rest of the way, but my legs hung from my torso like concrete poles. Soon we arrived at the young man's home. They exchanged some words about the next day's work, and then the young man got out and I took the front seat. We watched him walk to his building and waited until he let himself in. I wondered if Ned Frost was looking at his ass. "He's not going to work out," he said with genuine disappointment, driving off. "It's too bad, but he just doesn't have the patience for it. Cartography is a job of patience, really."

"That's true," I said.

At this, Ned laughed heartily, taking his hands off the steering wheel and rubbing his palms together. Then he was silent, brooding. He drove slowly. Finally, he said, "I was actually thinking about calling to see whether you'd be interested in working in the office again." He stopped at the light and said deliberately, "There is work. You know how to do the work. The work is what speaks."

I wondered, if I accepted his offer, whether he would still give me letters; I wondered if the letters were worth it for the job; I wondered if he expected me to sleep with him. He spoke with great enthusiasm about all the upcoming projects, and by the time we had arrived at my apartment building, I had agreed to take the job. I would start the following week, and Ned Frost would drive me to and from work as long as the strike lasted. He even offered to pay me more money. "There is money. The money is what speaks."

We got out of the car in front of my stoop, and Ned opened the trunk. He took out a few brochures. "Your maps," he said.

I peered at them under the feeble streetlight. They were for various things like an art fair and a business district. I ran my hand over the glossy covers and then flipped through until I found colorful images of my work.

"Nice, huh?" he said.

"Nice," I said. I handed them back.

"No, no, take them, Rex," Ned said. "Keep them. They're yours."

"Thanks," I said, and put them in my pocket.

"See you Monday," he said.

"See you Monday," I said.

We shook hands, and then I grabbed Ned Frost by his jacket and pushed him. Not hard, but enough to startle him and send him stumbling backward. There was a pause as he caught his breath and righted himself, and then I grabbed his jacket again, but this time I pulled him. For being so overweight he was surprisingly light, as if made of air, and I think his feet might have even come off the ground. His bearded face was inches from mine and I could smell his breath. I pitched him from side to side, as if rocking a boat for fun, and when I let go, he went off spinning toward the ground, grunting as he landed. A small notebook and pen came out of his pocket and rolled out into the empty street. This made me feel sad, and I went and picked them up and brought them back to him. "Here you go," I said.

He was on all fours breathing hard, the white breath coming out in bursts from his mouth and nose. I set the notebook and pen down beside him and waited until he had brought himself to a standing position. He brushed off his pants. His tweed jacket had torn in the armpit, and I wondered if he'd notice that before he wore it again, or if someone would point it out to him at work. He stooped down and picked up his pen and pad and put them back in his pocket. Once he had oriented himself, he got back in his car without looking at me. I watched him sit there for a while collecting himself, and then he drove off down the street.

That night Frankie and I were eating pizza when the basketball game was interrupted by a local news report telling us that the bus strike was over. The state supreme court had ordered the drivers back to work immediately, contract or no contract. There was a clip of the mayor saying that he felt great relief that the city would finally get itself back on its feet.

"The drivers," Frankie said, "the drivers . . . they . . . got screwed!"

Then the basketball game came on again.

On Monday the buses were up and running. I woke early to the sound of a diesel engine just below my window. I got dressed and went downstairs to see for myself. Fifteen minutes later, sure enough, a bus came rolling around the corner and stopped and opened its doors for me. "This ride's on us," read a sign taped over the fare box. The driver looked as if the sign might as well have been hanging around his neck. The bus was full with everyone trying to get to work. I found a seat in the back and looked out the window as the bus crawled past the playground and the laundromat and the Buy 'n' Save. We made a right turn, stopped to pick up some more passengers, and then headed onto the thoroughfare. I had nowhere to go, of course, but for a moment it felt as if I were free.

PARANOIA

When April arrived, it started to get warm and everyone said that the war was definitely going to happen soon and there was nothing anybody could do to stop it. The diplomats were flying home, the flags were coming out, and the call-ups were about to begin. Walking across the bridge, I would sometimes see freight trains lumbering by, loaded top to bottom with tanks or jeeps, once even the wings of airplanes, heading out west or down south. Some line had been crossed, something said or done, something irrevocable on our side or on the enemy's, from which there was no longer any possibility of turning back. I hadn't been following matters that closely, so I had missed exactly when things had taken a turn. Nevertheless, everyone was saying that the war was going to happen soon and so I said it too.

Then May came and it got hot and Roberto broke his nose

and asked me if I would come visit him in the hospital. "Blood everywhere," he told me over the phone. Apparently he had been lifting weights at the gym when one of his buddies, in order to emphasize some conversational point he was making, feinted like a boxer and swung at Roberto's face. The buddy had meant merely to pantomime the punch, but with his arms heavy-light from having just bench-pressed three hundred pounds, he had lost the ability to gauge distance, strength, or speed, and he cracked Roberto right in the nose. I wanted to question the details of the story because Roberto was subject to hyperbole, and also because I was selfish and didn't want to make the trip across town, but I was the closest thing to family that Roberto had, and on the telephone he did sound like he had a sock stuffed down his throat and up his nose.

To make matters worse, my car happened to be in the shop, and according to the bus map, I had to catch three buses I'd never heard of. So what should have taken me twenty minutes was going to take an hour and a half. Sitting in the back of the J-23B with the air-conditioning barely working, I stared out the window as we crawled through residential neighborhoods whose houses were all hung with flags. There was no breeze, and the flags hung limply. Some of the homes displayed the MIA and POW flags from bygone wars, and every so often there'd be a sign stuck in a window that said PEACE or NO WAR or something to that effect, but those were few and far between, and for the most part everyone was on the same page. Ten minutes into the ride, I was sweating heavily; rivulets ran from my armpits down my sides and collected in the elastic of my underwear. This is what it must feel like for soldiers on the transport heading to battle, I thought. I was wearing shorts and my thighs adhered to the bus seat so that whenever I shifted, my skin peeled away from the plastic. The other passengers were old hands and obviously knew what was in store for them because they'd come equipped with things to fan themselves, things like newspapers and magazines and even a flattened cereal box. Out of the corner of my eye, the rapid motion resembled birds alighting. Twenty-five minutes into the ride, I retrieved a discarded supermarket circular from under the seat in from of me and tried to use it as a fan, but the paper was too thin and kept flopping over and I wasn't able to generate any current. I folded it four times and then gave up and tossed it back under the seat where I'd found it. A woman looked at me with disapproval. She was waving a book in front of her face.

"It was already on the floor," I said. I smiled.

She shrugged. She didn't care.

At every corner, the bus hit a red light, and we'd have to sit idling for sixty seconds, stewing in the pot, and then once the light turned green and the bus made it through the intersection, it would stop again to let passengers on and off, elderly people who took forever, fat people who took forever, a man in a wheelchair who took five minutes, and by the time we arrived at the end of the next block, the light would be turning red again and we'd have to stop and idle and do the whole thing all over. It was abysmal urban planning, humiliating and crushing. I kept urging the bus forward by tensing and twisting and leaning forward like a bowler who imagines his body language can influence the trajectory of the ball once it's left his hand. My skin peeled. I blamed everyone: the bus, the driver, the passengers. I blamed Roberto for breaking his nose. Then I blamed myself for blaming Roberto. It wasn't his fault. Nothing was his fault. His nose was just another symptom of his vulnerability, his desperation, a strange man in a strange land, hoping one day to magically transform into an American and have a real life. "I'm already an American," he'd say indignantly, haughtily, in a clipped and formal way that was supposed to emphasize the fact that he had lost, through extreme effort, all traces of an accent. "I'm an American just like you!" But he wasn't just like me. He was dark—dark-skinned, dark-haired, black-eyed, from some village that nobody had ever heard of and which he'd left twelve years earlier when his father was awarded a scholarship to study architecture at our university, all expenses paid.

I had discovered him in the park one afternoon about two weeks after he arrived, thirteen years old, skinny and solitary, unable to speak a word of English, tossing a baseball up in the air. "*¿Te gusta jugar al beisbol?*" I'd said, because I'd been taking Spanish for two years, though the teacher, despite providing us with an extensive vocabulary and showing us how to conjugate every verb backward and forward, had neglected to teach us how to construct a complete sentence save one: "Do you like to play baseball?" Roberto had gazed at me in confusion, almost terror, until finally he responded, "*Sí, me gusta jugar al beisbol.*" Four years later, his father graduated with honors and the family's visa expired, effective immediately. It was time to go back. But Roberto had no interest in going back. So they went back without him, leaving him with eight months of high school to go, alone and illegal, in an apartment that had been emptied of almost everything, including the furniture. I was there the day after they left. It looked like it had been ransacked. He had his bed and his clothes, but that was about it. The closets were open and empty, and the curtains were gone. Standing in the void of a three-bedroom apartment he couldn't pay for, he tried to act chipper about his prospects at age seventeen. In his newfound independence, he had taken the opportunity to cut out pictures of Arnold Schwarzenegger at various stages of his career and paste them on the wall like wallpaper. There was nothing in the refrigerator except a jar of mayonnaise and a can of tuna fish, but it didn't matter, because he didn't have any dishes.

A few blocks from the infamous Maple Tree Heights, I had to transfer to the K-4AB. It was just pulling away when I arrived. I chased after it as it sailed down the street. Some elderly black women passed me pushing shopping carts, and one said, "That's a shame, honey," and another said, "That's how they do you up here." At the end of the street was a hill with a sharp ascent, and a billboard that read, WELCOME TO MAPLE TREE HEIGHTS. The billboard looked brand-new except for the fact that someone had crawled up and spray-painted, "Don't come on in here." Every week there was a report on the news of some unfortunate event, many involving white people who had lost their way and wound up wandering through Maple Tree Heights, where they were set upon and beaten for sport. Most recently a mathematics professor had been whipped with a snakeskin belt. I reflected on how the scrawled message could be interpreted less as implied threat and more as honest warning. It also seemed possible that the message was not being directed outward at all but inward, at those who already lived in Maple Tree Heights and might be contemplating moving to some other part of the city.

It was ten o'clock in the morning and already muggy, slushy, the air slow-moving. "Hitting ninety today, folks," the weatherman had said. Everyone was saying that if it was ninety in May, what was it going to be in August. The sky was cloudless, and I could feel the undiluted sun beating straight down on the top of my head. There were various empty buildings surrounding me, and I had the sensation that I was being watched by someone somewhere. I felt exposed in my shorts, my whiteness made manifest by the paleness of my legs. Directly across the street was an Arby's with an American flag draped across its giant cowboy hat. I should go inside to wait for the bus, I thought. I'll be safe there. But as soon as I thought this, three black guys about my age came out of the restaurant with their roast-beef-sandwich bags and big boots and baseball caps and stood underneath the hat, smoking and staring at me. I put my hands in my pockets casually and looked up the street as if I were fixated on what was coming. Nothing was coming. The empty air wobbled in the heat. When I glanced back, the guys were still smoking and saying things to one another, low things, conspiratorial things. They had expertly tilted their baseball caps down so that I couldn't see where precisely they were looking, but I knew they were looking at me. I thought about running, but running implied terror. Or capitulation. For a moment I had a clear picture of myself disoriented, panting, turning in error up into Maple Tree Heights.

Then I heard my name being called. "Dean!" I heard. "Goddamn, Dean!"

When I looked back at the three guys, I saw that they were smiling and that I knew them, two of them; we had played together on the football team in high school. And here they came from underneath the Arby's hat, laughing, yelling, their bags of roast-beef sandwiches in one hand, their cigarettes in the other. "Goddamn, Dean," they said. "How long's it been?" There was some initial awkwardness as we tried to coordinate the hand slapping and the hugging and the sandwiches and the cigarettes, but eventually we managed to greet one another properly.

I introduced myself to the one I didn't know.

"What's up, my man?" he said. He looked skeptical.

"We thought you were the police," Quincy said.

This made everyone laugh. The man I didn't know laughed bitterly, and I laughed out of relief at this fortunate turn of events. Troy blew smoke out of his nose, and Quincy blew it out of his mouth, and I wanted to ask for a cigarette, because I was eager to fortify our bond and because I only smoke when I can smoke for free. The man I didn't know removed a handkerchief and wiped his forehead. Then he took out his sandwich and bit into it, and I could smell the roast beef, which in the heat made me queasy.

"What are you doing all the way out here, Dean?" Quincy wanted to know. "This here is no-man's-land."

"I'm waiting for the bus," I said. "I'm on my way to see Robbie."

"Robbie?"

"Robbie Díaz?"

"Spanish Robbie?"

"Goddamn, man!"

"How's Robbie?"

"He broke his nose."

"That ain't cool."

"Tell him I said what's up."

"Bus?" said the man I didn't know. "There ain't no bus here."

I pointed to the sign above my head.

"There ain't no bus here," he repeated. He was the kind of person who offered the minimum amount of information possible.

"Bus stop is over there," Quincy said. He pointed up the street to an abandoned building with broken windows and a sign that said TEXTILES Something-or-other, INC. The words had eroded.

"Hey, Troy," I said. "How about letting me have one of those cigarettes?"

Troy aimed his pack in my direction, and out popped a cigarette halfway. A surge of nostalgia and tenderness coursed through me for our old football games. I put the cigarette to my lips with great anticipation, but Troy's matches were moist or stale, and each time I struck one, it would flare up for a second and then fizzle out. After the third miss, I asked the man I didn't know if I could use his lighter. He handed it to me grudgingly. It had a picture of an American flag on it. When I flicked the lighter, the flag fluttered as if waving in the wind.

"Let me see that," Quincy said, and we passed the lighter around, flicking it on and off, marveling at the trick, until the man I didn't know said not to waste any more fluid.

"I was just thinking about getting me a tattoo like that," Troy announced. "Right here." He pulled up his shirt to reveal a saggy and swollen stomach. "Here to here." He outlined the image like a teacher standing at a chalkboard. "Here's where the flagpole goes." He indicated his belly button.

"That would look good," I said, but I didn't think it would look good. I was dismayed by what had become of his body. He was round and spongy, as if he had rolled in a pan of chocolate dough. So was Quincy. The man I didn't know was the opposite, tall and stringy, with ropy muscles and long fingers and protruding knuckles. He was thin but sweating the most. Sweat streamed down from under his baseball cap, and he dabbed at it with his handkerchief. He was oddly genteel about this. Then he cracked his knuckles loudly, aggressively, and it made a sound like tree branches snapping. Troy pulled his shirt back down, and I had a vivid recollection of him standing in front of the locker-room mirror after one of our games, completely naked except for his socks, flexing and preening. At fifteen, he already had a man's body—shoulders, chest, and cock. He'd scored three touchdowns that game and knocked the opposing team's star player unconscious. Coach Slippo had given him the game ball. He had five game balls. "I've got some cuts in here for you," Troy had told the equipment manager, running his fingers through the creases of his stomach muscles and down to the edge of his pelvis. Everyone had laughed. The equipment manager had blushed. Troy thought he was going to make the NFL. All of the guys thought they were going to make the NFL. They didn't even make college.

I sucked the smoke in and blew it out, and as I did, it felt like my mouth was a furnace door that I was opening. The smoke was hotter than the air, and it made my face fiery and my eyes water. I felt light-headed, and the smell of the roast beef was sickening. There was a thrumming in my eardrums. I feared I might puke on the sidewalk.

"You okay, Dean?" I heard Troy say. "You good?" His voice was far away. I wasn't sure if he was asking whether my life in general was good.

"It's hot out here," I said. It was all I could do to maintain my balance.

"This ain't hot," said the man I didn't know. "If you think this is hot, wait till August."

I was happy to engage in weather talk. "It's probably going to be a hundred degrees in August," I offered.

"A hundred degrees?" The man I didn't know was incredulous. "A hundred degrees?" He was outraged. He looked at me hard. "If it's ninety degrees in May, how's it going to be a hundred degrees in August? I'm telling you, my man, it's going to be hundred and *twenty-five* degrees in August."

Against my better judgment, I took another drag off the cigarette, and it had a surprising calming effect. The smoke came out white and round and hovered around my head in the still, heavy air.

"Hey, Dean," Quincy said suddenly, "you looking for a job?"

Troy said, "Dean don't need no job."

"They're hiring," Quincy said. He nodded to the textiles building down the street.

"Who's hiring?" I said.

"Mainframes, man," Quincy said.

"Chemicals and whatnot," Troy said.

"I don't ask no questions about what they make," said the man I didn't know.

"You watch," Quincy said. "Once the war starts, they'll be opening factories all up and down this street. There's going to be an industrial revolution right here in the ghetto." This broke them up. They slapped one another's hands, stinging slaps. I smiled but I didn't slap.

"Where you working at now, Dean?" Troy said.

I told him.

"Damn."

"Damn."

"That's a good job."

"How'd you get that?"

"That's the kind of gig I want."

"Damn."

"That's what I'm going to get me," said the man I didn't know. He said this more to himself. Then he said to the rest of us, "I'm going to get one of those *essential* jobs, so that when the draft comes, they pass me up."

"There's not going to be any draft," I said. It was my turn to state something as fact.

The man looked at me in astonishment. He cocked his head. Then he guffawed and wiped his handkerchief over his entire face in one swift motion. "How'd you figure that one out, my man?"

"It's going to be a quick war," I said. "Marines are going to take the peninsula first thing." I drew in the air as if I was standing in front of a map. "Here's the bay . . . here's the peninsula . . . you'll see."

The guys got quiet as they pondered this.

"Anyway," I said cheerfully, "even if it's a long war, there'll still be plenty of people willing to join up."

"Plenty of *people*?" The man I didn't know snorted. "This here's the guy"—he turned to Troy and Quincy—"who thinks it's only going to be a hundred degrees in August."

At the hospital, the air-conditioning was going full blast and the sweat froze on my skin. It was almost twelve o'clock and I was exhausted and parched. I was also hungry. I went back to blaming Roberto for everything. People with all sorts of ailments came and went in the waiting room, and I thought about how this must be what it's like when soldiers get back from battle. I wasn't sure if Roberto had checked in under a false name. He was nervous about not being a citizen and was always going out of his way to cover his tracks. He had no driver's license, no bank account, no telephone, and his new apartment still had the name of the previous tenant, Cynthia Abernathy, on the mailbox even though she hadn't lived there for two years. Every so often he'd get a package for her, and he'd tell the delivery guy some elaborate and unnecessary story about how Cynthia was his wife but she was out of town because her mother was dying and he didn't know when she'd be back but he'd let her know that a package had come for her when he talked to her next but he wasn't sure when that would be because her mother was dying. It was always the same story. He was positive that the INS was tracking him and the delivery guy was an agent. In the meantime, he'd accumulated several mail-order kitchen gadgets, including an electric egg-beater.

"Don't you think they're going to start wondering why your mother-in-law never dies?" I'd ask him.

He never liked this. "You're going to be *penitent* one day," he'd say, dropping in one of those words he'd learned specifically for the SAT. "You're going to be *penitent* when they come for me. They're going to lock me up somewhere, like they did those apple pickers, and you're never going to hear from me again."

"I'm looking for Roberto Díaz," I told the hospital receptionist.

She checked the computer. No, she said, there was no Roberto Díaz listed.

"Then I'm looking for Rob Days," I said.

No, sorry.

"How about Bob Hays?" I was trying to recall all the various permutations he had used over the years.

No.

"I'm looking for Tyler McCoy," I said, because this was the name of the main character in his favorite gangster film.

The receptionist punched in Tyler McCoy, and I could tell by the way she slowly struck the keys that she was getting suspicious or impatient. "You sure do have a lot of friends," she said.

"I sure do," I said. And Tyler McCoy was in Room 831.

He was asleep when I got there, lying on his back with his mouth wide open like a drowning man trying to suck oxygen. He had bandages running ear to ear, and his nose, always prominent, seemed gigantic under the bandages, as if he had an anvil for a nose. His eyes were swollen, his hair was matted, and a *Reader's Digest* rested on his stomach, rising and falling with his haggard breath. Across the room a window faced out onto the roof of an adjacent wing of the hospital. The roof was white, and if you didn't know it was ninety degrees outside, you could mistake the whiteness for snow.

I pulled up a chair next to his bed and took a seat. He didn't stir. I thought about turning on the television and then, when he woke, apologizing for having disturbed him. From my vantage point, he looked to be all torso, as if he were lying in bed after having had his legs amputated. This was a result of having spent ten years lifting weights constantly and incorrectly. I'd experienced him straining, screaming, staggering, a terrifying sight to behold as he attempted to hoist more than was humanly possible, and the second the summit was attained, not one second more, he would discard the barbell midair so that it would drop and crash and bounce in explosive vanity. His chest was colossal and so were his shoulders and his arms, and he had a thick blue vein in his neck that was permanently engorged as it piped gallons of blood to his muscles twenty-four hours a day. But his legs were thin, the legs of a teenage girl or an insect, and they looked nonexistent beneath the pale blue hospital sheet. "Why don't you try doing some cardio every once in a while?" I'd counsel. He either didn't care or didn't notice that his proportions bordered on the freakish. His physique had provided him with those coveted manual-labor jobs—mover, deliverer, unloader—and that was how he had survived all these years without any aid or assistance except what he got from me. Businesses needed men like him and were happy to pay him under the table. He'd carried bricks, drywall, bales of hay. "I've got a special job for Robbie," my mother once said. He'd come over for dinner and wound up spending half an hour lugging a tree trunk from our backyard to the curb. She'd given him ten dollars. I'd yelled at her later for what I saw as an example of her condescension, but my father intervened, coming into the living room in his bare feet and no glasses and uttering one of his platitudes, "Every man has to make his own way in this world."

The way Roberto was making his own way in this world now was through relatively sedentary employment as an assistant to a cobbler who also happened to be his landlord and who cut him a break on the rent in addition to giving him shoes if they were left in the shop past sixty days. Roberto would be turning twenty-five soon, and he'd come up with a fairly reasonable plan that involved learning a trade, saving money, going to college, opening a business, starting a family. The cobbler paid him in cash twice a month, so twice a month he had an enormous roll of money that he liked to caress as if it were a puppy. The roll was generally in fives and tens and added up to no more than a couple hundred dollars, but it made him look and feel rich. "Like Tyler McCoy," he'd say, and he'd reenact in pitch-perfect detail the scene where Tyler McCoy is trying to get one guy to go in with another guy on the heist that turned out to be a double cross. "Me. You. Now. Together." When Roberto had satisfied himself with fondling the roll, we would walk to the post office, where he would buy all the money orders he needed to pay all the bills that were under assumed names. We'd wait in a long line of poor people and illegal immigrants and that occasional unfortunate American citizen who had just come in to buy a book of stamps. When we emerged from the post office an hour later, Roberto would be broke.

The mass of flesh suddenly shifted like an animal beneath forest leaves, and his swollen eyes opened. They were bloodshot and bleary, and it took a moment for him to orient himself. "Oh, shit," he said when he understood who I was and where we were. "You came. My man." His voice was thick and stuffy like air in a cellar, and I was surprised to hear the slightest trace of the accent he had rid himself of years ago. It could have been an earlier version of him rising from the dead. *Oh, shee. You came. My main.*

"Of course I came," I said, wounded, as if I had never contemplated otherwise. And because I knew it would make him happy and endear me to him, I added, "Of course I came, *Tyler.*"

He grinned, and the bandages pulled tight across his face, and the grin evaporated as he cried out in agony. I stood in alarm, but the pain subsided quickly. He struggled out of bed, throwing the sheet back with determination, bringing both feet to the floor and forcing himself upright so that he could face me.

"This is the best guy," he said with the utmost sincerity, as if introducing me to an audience. "This is the greatest guy in the whole world." This was an example of Roberto's hyperbole.

His trunklike arms came around my shoulders and squeezed me hard, until I felt like a child, even though I was taller than he was. I feared he would lift me off the ground and swing me. Instead, he laid his head against my chest, so that he was the one who seemed transformed into a boy, hugging his father the day before he left for good.

In June, the marines were put on high alert, the temperature reached one hundred degrees, and the bill from the hospital arrived. It was three thousand dollars.

I loaned Roberto two hundred to cover the minimum, and a few days later he called me from the cobbler's phone to invite me over to his apartment to see his "special surprise."

"What special surprise is that?" I said, but he refused to tell me. He had to get back to work.

So the following Saturday, which also turned out to be the hottest day of the year so far, I pulled up to his apartment building. It was early evening, but it seemed to be getting hotter, as if the setting sun were drawing nearer. Roberto lived in one of those neighborhoods that were either up-and-coming or on the way out, an equal mix of aluminum siding, college students, and small shops—one of which was the cobbler's shop, whose awning I now stood beneath, waiting desperately for Roberto to come downstairs and let me in. His doorbell never worked but I had been forbidden by the cobbler to yell up at the window. Instead, I had to arrive at our mutually agreed-upon time and stand on the sidewalk patiently and quietly until Roberto opened the door. If I showed up early, I'd have to wait; if I showed up late, Roberto would have to wait. Today I showed up right on time, but there was no Roberto. Every few minutes, behind the window, the cobbler would rise from his shoe machine and eye me mercilessly, as if he'd never seen me before and suspected I was up to no good. He hated me, and I hated him. He was fat, and he smoked constantly, and he had a thick head of black hair. I had a theory that he colored it with shoe polish. He was Italian or Greek or Armenian—we could never figure out which—and he had been in America for fifty years but could hardly speak English. Even Roberto made fun of him. "'I can no find a-black-a shoelazes . . .'" I'd gotten off to a bad start with him the first time I visited Roberto and screamed up at the window at eleven o'clock in the morning, "*Robbie!*"

"You no come here act like hoodlum," the cobbler had demanded. "Like nigger."

"Hey!"

"Hey!"

"That word's not called for!"

"I call police!"

"Fix the doorbell!"

"I fix you!"

"Fuck off!"

"That word not called for!"

"He's my window of opportunity," Roberto had shrieked when I told him what happened. So I went back downstairs, hat in hand, and apologized.

"My customers good customers" was all he said.

Fifteen minutes after I had arrived, Roberto still hadn't come down to open the door. This wasn't like him at all, and a subtle unease began to creep over me. I recalled the apple pickers who had been rounded up by the INS in the middle of the night, and I was on the verge of panicking when Roberto appeared from around the corner, carrying a big blue box that said DVD PLAYER. He was grinning freely, despite his nose being covered with bandages that made it look as if he had a small pillow in the middle of his face.

"What's in the box?" I said, though it was obvious what was in the box.

"Robbie!" said the cobbler, waving. "You buy me DVD player?"

Roberto laughed, and so did the cobbler. The cobbler's laugh was intended to make me the odd man out.

In his apartment Roberto sat cross-legged on the floor, tearing open the box as if it were Christmas Day. Styrofoam peanuts went everywhere, and when he removed the thin silver DVD player, it gleamed sharply in the evening light. He smiled at it lovingly. I sat on the sofa and fumed, dripping with sweat. His apartment was even hotter than outside. It was one square room with a kitchenette, a saggy sofa bed, and three folding chairs; the bathroom was down the hall and shared with six other tenants. All Roberto's furniture belonged to the cobbler, and so did the television and dishes. The wall of his kitchenette had been covered meticulously with those pictures of Arnold Schwarzenegger, the most prominent of which was him in a suit and tie with his arms and thighs pressing hard against the fabric. The apartment felt like a boiler room in a sub-subbasement. It even sounded like a boiler room, with the constant low-frequency vibration coming from the cobbler's shoe machine. Roberto seemed wholly unaffected by the heat. He was always unaffected by the heat. I had never seen him sweat.

"Can't you open a window?" I asked.

With one gigantic arm, he swung open the window and then got back to fitting inputs into outputs. Immediately a fly came in through the window, but no breeze. I watched the fly settle on a plate and crawl around. Then a second fly came in. Roberto turned on the television to a game show that was nearing its climax. A woman had to pick the right color if she wanted to win fifty thousand dollars. The audience was screaming at her, and she was flustered.

"What will you do with *all that money*?" the host asked.

"I-I-I-I don't know."

"Pay back the greatest guy," I answered for her.

"What?" Roberto said. His pillow face swung in my direction.

"Pay back the greatest guy in the whole world," I said.

He stood up straight. In his small apartment, his size was immense, his camel legs notwithstanding, and as he loomed over me on the couch, I felt a twinge of vulnerability.

"I told you, I'm going to pay you every penny!" he said. His face twitched and the pillow-bandage bobbed, and from his pocket he withdrew a slip of paper on which was printed the company logo of Dr. Scholl's. Beneath this he had written in very precise handwriting, "I O Dean $200.00." He had dated it "June 14th" and added his initials, as if it were an official document he was endorsing. The gesture was surprisingly touching, and I felt remorseful, even guilty, as if I were the one who owed money.

Out loud I said, "What the hell am I supposed to do with this? Get it notarized?"

"Motorized?" he asked.

He shrugged. He folded the paper and put it in his pocket and got back to work on the DVD player. The woman was just about to pick the color yellow when the game show was interrupted by breaking news: every branch of the military had been ordered to join the marines on high alert—the navy, the army, the air force, the coast guard, and branches I'd never heard of. There were maps with arrows, and the peninsula was highlighted. The experts were all in agreement; even the experts who used to disagree now agreed. Everything made sense. There was a sexy reporter interviewing soldiers at their base.

"We could be attacked without warning," she said. "Right here and now." Her eyes were dewy, her lips were thick. She wore a flak jacket and a helmet from under which flowed long brown hair.

"Do you miss your family?" she asked one of the soldiers.

"Yes, I do, ma'am," the soldier said.

Roberto came and sat beside me on the sofa.

"But I have to do what I have to do," the soldier said. He had blond hair, blue eyes, an upturned nose. If not for his twang, he could have been a California surfer. Night-vision goggles were propped on his forehead.

"Are you afraid of dying?"

"No, ma'am."

"Any day now," the reporter said, turning to us.

"Any day now," Roberto repeated. The sentiment seemed poignant. I draped my arm around his enormous shoulders. I was in a forgiving mood.

"Let's go get a DVD," I said.

Outside, the cobbler was closing up for the night. He was trying to pull the grate down over the shopwindow but was having trouble because he was old and fat. Roberto ran to his aid as if rescuing a child from the water's edge. "Wait! Wait! Stop! Stop!" He reached up with wide forearms, and in an instant the gate came crashing down onto the boiling sidewalk.

"Ah, you good man," the cobbler said.

At the video store we browsed the titles. We agreed, finally, on one of those funny buddy road movies. Then Roberto picked a porno that he said he was going to watch alone. And then he picked his favorite gangster movie with Tyler McCoy.

I paid for all three.

Back at the apartment, there were about forty flies walking over everything, including the dishes.

"Maybe you should close the window," I suggested.

He complied, trapping the heat and trapping the flies. Then he went to the refrigerator and took out some bread and cheese and tuna fish and put them on the counter where the flies were. He took out a jar of mayonnaise, and while his back was turned, the flies landed on the bread and cheese and tuna fish. When he was done making the sandwiches, he put one on a plate where the flies had been and handed it to me.

He sat down on the sofa bed and pressed play. The trailers ran and the sofa sagged. After that, the movie with Tyler McCoy began. I pressed pause.

"I thought we were going to watch the other one," I said. "The buddy one."

"Let's watch this one first."

"I've seen it three times," I said.

"So what," he said, "I've seen it three *hundred* times." This was no exaggeration.

He pressed play, and so began Tyler McCoy's rags-to-riches story through violent and immoral means. When the characters spoke, Roberto spoke, every word, soundlessly mouthing in perfect unison.

He pressed pause. "Why aren't you eating your sandwich?" he asked.

"I think I saw a fly land on it," I admitted.

With irritation he said, "You are *opulent*," and he took the sandwich from me and bit into it, a huge, obvious bite so that I could see the food in his mouth. "And I am *indigent*."

Which was true. I'd had a DVD player for ten years.

On the Fourth of July, Roberto and I drove downtown to see the parade. There was nowhere to park, and we had to walk twenty minutes up a hill in 105-degree heat. The turnout was extraordinary. The largest ever, people were saying. Other people were saying that each year the turnout should be the largest ever and that people shouldn't wait for a war to be-come patriots. "I keep my flag out year-round," one man said. "And you can pass by my house anytime to see if I'm telling the truth." The fountain was going, though we were supposed to be conserving water, and the parks people had somehow managed to get it to rise and fall in alternating colors of red, white, and blue. Up and down it went, hypnotically. Roberto and I stood shoulder to shoulder, transfixed by the spectacle. Children played along the edge, and parents screamed at them not to drink the water because it was poisonous.

The sun was straight overhead, but the heat felt as if it were coming from down below, from the asphalt, emanating up through my shoes and legs and out through my scalp. I had brought along a container of sunblock, SPF 45, which I kept applying to my face and neck every few minutes. Roberto looked at me in fascination and amusement. His nose was almost healed except for a small red mark that ran along the bridge and which he kept rubbing because he was self-conscious.

"Does my nose look big?" he asked.

"Not at all," I lied.

"Ladies and gentlemen," the emcee said, and a band started up, all trumpets and drums and tubas playing "My Country, 'Tis of Thee." People swayed and sang, and Roberto used the heartfelt moment as an opportunity to make his first payment. "To the best friend," he announced, holding a pile of crumpled bills. "To the greatest friend in the whole world." He handed over the fistful of dollars like he was pouring gold coins into my hands. "Count," he said.

I counted twenty dollars.

He displayed the sheet of paper with the Dr. Scholl's logo and his now updated balance sheet. He had crossed out "I O Dean $200.00" and replaced it with "I O Dean $180.00, RD," dated "July 4th."

I used some of the money to treat us to two foot-longs, and I was about to treat us to two more when an altercation broke out near the fountain. People pushed to get to the action, and Roberto and I pushed too, and the emcee said not to push. The crowd surged forward, and when the wall of people opened, I could see parade-goers shouting and pointing at a small ragtag group of protesters holding signs that said WAR IS NOT THE ANSWER and things of that nature.

We jeered at them, and they jeered back. "You're all fools," they screamed.

"It's the Fourth of July, for crying out loud," a woman next to me yelled back. Her face was pink, possibly burning, and she looked close to tears. "Isn't anything sacred to you people?"

Roberto cupped his hands around his mouth and bellowed, "Faggots!"

People laughed.

"Hey," I hissed at Roberto. "That word's not called for!"

Some of the parade-goers began splashing the protesters with blue water from the fountain, and soon the police arrived to separate everyone and escort the protesters to a special section at the other end of the park. The band struck up the national anthem. We put our hands over our hearts as veterans from previous wars began marching past, starting with World War II. There were only a few of these, and they ambled by slowly, looking confused and displaced, their uniforms baggy like diapers and draped with medals that glinted in the sun. Their children and grandchildren and maybe great-grandchildren helped them along and did the waving for them. People applauded, but the applause seemed to disorient the veterans. "Thank you," Roberto called, "thank you for all you've done!"

As the wars progressed, the soldiers got younger, until we arrived at the youngest, the new recruits. By the time they appeared, I was exhausted from the heat and the clapping. I felt like I was being immersed in boiling water, and I was sure I had a terrible burn on the back of my neck. Still, I mustered the energy and pounded my hands harder than I had up to that point. This was bon voyage for the new recruits—they were marching from the parade straight to the train depot. "Last stop, the peninsula," the emcee said. The crowd went wild. Roberto and I clapped harder yet. The soldiers came marching down in lines of twenty. Line after line. Ten minutes of lines. A mass of bodies larger than the crowd watching. They were decked out in the latest gear, everything streamlined and advanced: goggles and helmets, tool belts and boots, lights and antennas. They resembled astronauts with automatic weapons.

"To the moon!" I yelled. It had a nice ring to it.

"To the moon!" Roberto yelled.

And then I saw a familiar face. I couldn't place the face, but I knew that I knew it. I knew it vaguely. The man was tall and frail, and the helmet looked too large for his head, more like a bonnet than a helmet, and with each step it bobbled and appeared in danger of slipping off. He fumbled with the strap, trying to tighten it and keep pace at the same time. Sweat poured down his face as if he'd just climbed out of a swimming pool. He seemed on the verge of collapse.

"I know that man," I said.

"Thank you," Roberto shouted.

The man reached into one of the many pockets on his jacket and withdrew a handkerchief. In one clean motion, he brought the handkerchief down across his dripping face. Then he turned and looked at me. *The man I didn't know.*

"Hey," I called. I smiled and waved.

He squinted. He seemed to be looking at me and then beyond me. The attitude of haughty disdain that he'd had that day at the bus stop had been replaced by a look of fatigue and befuddlement. I wondered if Quincy and Troy were with him, and I scrutinized the lines of marching soldiers. An instant later, the man I didn't know had passed, and all I could see was his back, with his enormous pack weighed down by the essentials and an antenna sticking out.

I cried out after him, "I told you there wasn't going to be a draft!"

In August something strange happened: it got cold. In one day, it plummeted from a record high of 107 to 95 degrees. This felt like relief. But after that the temperature kept dropping, until by the middle of the month it was fifty-three. In the beginning of the cold snap, everyone was happy, and then everyone was scared. Everyone was saying that if it was fifty degrees in August, what was it going to be in December.

Things got busy at work and I didn't see Roberto for a while. We made plans and I canceled plans, and then we made plans again. He said he really wanted to watch that funny buddy road movie we never got to watch. He said he had my money. All of it. Or almost all of it. I wanted to tell him not to worry about it, that it didn't matter, but it did matter, and I rationalized that paying me back would help teach him something about responsible American citizenship.

We finally arranged to meet on Saturday morning at ten o'clock.

The night before, I was lying in bed, watching the news about some bad things that had happened in Maple Tree Heights, when it was interrupted by a special report: the war had begun. The invasion was being broadcast live, lots of lights and flashes and little bursts of smoke from afar. *Rat-a-tat-tat*. Instead of troops landing on the peninsula, as we had been led to believe, they were coming down over the mountains. The peninsula strategy had all been a deft misdirection to fool the enemy. Ten thousand feet high, the mountains were. Up one side and down the other, a hundred thousand troops on the move. It was going to take them a week to make the crossing. What was it like, I wondered, to reach the summit?

I stayed up late, flipping back and forth between channels. The channels all showed the same footage, and all the experts agreed: "Resistance was futile."

"Ladies and gentlemen," the newscaster said, "blink and you might miss this war."

In the morning my car was broken again, it wouldn't start, and I had to walk to Roberto's. It was freezing. It might as well have been winter. The sun was hidden and the wind blew hard, whipping the flags around. People drove past me and honked in unity.

When I got to Roberto's apartment, I was numb. My nose was running and I had to pee. The gate to the cobbler's was up, but the shop looked unattended. I pounded my hands together and stomped my feet to get the blood going. Five minutes into waiting, I began to suspect that Roberto was about to come around the corner and "surprise" me with another box of electronics. Five minutes after that, I took my chances and shouted up to the window. "*Robbie!*"

Immediately the cobbler came out. He looked at me and sucked in the sides of his cheeks.

"The doorbell doesn't seem to be working," I said sarcastically.

He shook his head. "No talk here," he said. His eyes were tense and bloodshot, and he puffed hard on his cigarette. Smoke billowed out from all the orifices of his face. Beneath his apron, his stomach protruded, firm and round. "Come in store," he said. "No good talk out here."

I followed him inside. He put his cigarette in the ashtray and sat down at his machine as if he were about to get back to work. I leaned on the counter like a customer.

"Yesterday," he said as he rubbed his dirty hands over his face. "Yesterday they come." He wasn't looking at me as he spoke. Somehow his dirty hands hadn't made his face dirty.

"Who come?" I said.

"Oh, no," he said. He put his black palms up in defense. "I don't ask question."

"Who come?" I demanded.

He looked at me with trepidation. Slowly, stumblingly, full of error, he told me that yesterday they come for Roberto, yesterday, middle of day, four car, four car, no warning, all pull up same time, right outside, happen fast, take him way, take him. What I can do? I can do nothing. I am one man. They have law. Hurt me as much as hurt him.

He hunched his shoulders and he looked aggrieved. He was sorry, he said. "I pray for him now."

I believed him.

"He was nice boy," he said. "Hard worker. Hurt me too. Oh, boy." He ran his dirty fingers through his thick hair.

Then some people came in with their shoes, and he stood up to help them. His pack of cigarettes was on the counter, and I took one and stuck it in my mouth and lit it. He didn't notice. He didn't care. My boldness surprised me.

I took the long way home. I walked fast and hard. I smoked the cigarette, and the second I exhaled, the cold wind took the smoke. People drove past honking. I came down the hill and over the bridge. At the train tracks I stopped and tried to get my breath. I was wheezing. A small dot appeared way down the line. After a while it became a train. I could hear the rumble. When it drew closer, I could see that it was loaded with long tubular objects, missiles no doubt, twenty feet long, thirty feet, covered with canvas and strapped down with canvas belts. As the train approached, I saw the engineer hanging his head and arm out the window, and I motioned for him to pull the horn as I would have back when I was a kid. A moment later I heard the blast, *braaaaaammmmm;* it was louder than I had remembered, longer too, and then the train passed under the bridge as it headed out west or down south.

APPETITE

Things were not going as I had hoped. My sole purpose for interrupting my manager at this late hour on this Monday night was to inquire, respectfully, about an increase in my wage. But the conversation had somehow reversed itself, and now here I was standing awkwardly in the doorway of the restaurant office having to defend my very competency at my job. All through my shift I had entertained and distracted myself by imagining the scene in exacting detail: the gentle (or perhaps the assertive) knock on the office door, the disarming smile, the small talk about the weather, and then the casual introduction to the larger issue at hand, the larger issue that I had come to talk about with all reasonableness; the larger issue being eight to ten. That was how I had planned to say it: "I'm looking to move from eight to ten an hour." Simply put. Or perhaps, I'd thought, I would say, "I'm looking to move

to . . ." Or "I'm looking to move *up* to, up *from*, up *toward* . . ."
Somewhere I had heard that it's best to put your goals into
clear terms, straightforward terms, and that once those goals
had been thus stated, all would follow accordingly. In the rare
instance that things did not follow accordingly, the onus was,
of course, on you and your own ineptitude. I think I had heard
it discussed on television. Or I had read it somewhere. Or my
father had told me. The counsel had seemed wise at the time,
and I'd been determined to remember it if ever an occasion
presented itself.

So I stood in the doorway as my manager reclined in his
chair with his fingers to his chin, staring up at the dark skylight, where rain was pattering. It had rained every day for a
week. They said it was going to rain every day for another
week. Fall was always like this in our city. But this fall was
worse than others, they said. Soon it would be winter. "Business is bad, Ike," the manager had told me briskly, effortlessly,
as if he had been rehearsing the scene all night long also and
was waiting for me to ask so that he could answer and rid himself of the refrain in his head. Not knowing how to respond, I
said nothing, one foot crossed uncomfortably in front of the
other in what had been, initially, an attempt at bold informality
but, as time passed, quickly began to feel like an effeminate
posture that would help only in the case against my confidence
and assertiveness. And then my manager broke the awful silence by reminding me that two meals were returned by customers that evening. Why had two separate meals been
returned, he wanted to know. The clock on his desk read one
A.M. I wondered whether, if I had chosen to speak to him earlier that night, he would have been in a different mood, a more

conciliatory mood, and would not have dismissed my request so swiftly. Next to the clock were lists of the various ingredients that needed to be ordered; check marks in small boxes indicated the amounts. We dealt in volume: crates, jugs, sacks. The manager's pen was uncapped. His shirt was white except for a trail of red dots, presumably tomato sauce, running along one sleeve from elbow to shoulder. Or perhaps the dots were blood.

"A grilled cheese sandwich was returned tonight, Ike," my manager said. He stated it as if genuinely interested, philosophically speaking. "A grilled cheese sandwich and a plate of linguine. Why were they returned, Ike?"

I did not know why, and my face tightened with false concern. I realized that if I did not say something convincing, and say it fast, I would implicate myself by admitting not only that I had made defective, inedible food but that I had so little awareness of my job that I could not even recall why or when such an error had occurred. "I'll have to look into that" was all I said, as if I had my own underlings to consult. The clock now read 1:03. The manager's face was round and kind, with puffy cheeks, and in the office light it looked for some reason even kinder than usual. I should change the subject, I thought. And I should uncross my feet so that I don't look like a supplicant. I should talk about the rain and ask him when he thinks it will stop. It will make him think that I respect his authority. And then I will come back in a week and ask again for a raise—or in two weeks, maybe, not more than three, at some point in the near future, when everything has been forgotten and no meals have been returned and the rain has stopped and I have come up with a good response for when he tells me that business is bad.

But before I could say anything, my manager swiveled around in his chair, faced his desk, placed his hands lightly on top of the piles of paper there, as if they were a Ouija board and he was reading a signal from the beyond. Then he shuffled the papers around. Very rapidly, he shuffled the papers. "Seven-twenty-three the grilled cheese sandwich was returned," my manger read. "And eleven-fifty-two the plate of pasta came back."

Those times seemed so long ago. My manager looked up at me with his kind face, almost angelic. A baby face with puffy cheeks.

Answer him! But all I could think was that I was in the restaurant at 7:23. I was in the restaurant at 11:52. And here I am at 1:07, still in the restaurant. Tomorrow, I thought, I will be here. And the day after that. And the day after that is my day off. But then I will be back.

"Is it really that complicated, Ike, for you to make a grilled cheese sandwich?" the kind face asked.

Somewhere in my past, something had gone wrong for me. Years prior, at my high school graduation, I had sat docilely in the audience and watched the valedictorian onstage in a lavender cap and gown read a tedious and patronizing speech that I knew for a fact had been patched together from a book of stock lectures. "There are some of us here this evening who will be heading off to college," he declared, "others who are going into the military, and still others who are entering directly into the workforce." As if all those choices were equal. His voice, amplified by the microphone, sounded exceptionally powerful and confident, and I imagined that if he were to remove that ridiculous lavender gown, we would discover that he was naked underneath, and that he had, as I well knew from the locker room, broad shoulders and a broad chest and was not at all embarrassed to be seen naked. While beneath my billowy gown was a small-large frame, short legs but long arms, soft flesh but hard knees and elbows, with no real delineation between torso and limbs or between limbs and extremities: the body of a hamster. I was irritated by the valedictorian's speech and his three categories of life and his attempts at anecdotal humor that were supposed to seem spontaneous and ingratiate him with the parents but instead sounded contrived and wooden. The parents laughed and were won over. Sitting in the audience with five hundred other students, I had the unsettling awareness that I had already been consigned to a life of mediocrity by the very fact that I had not been the one chosen to stand on the podium. There was a single opportunity at having that happen in one's life, and I had missed it. Nothing could make up for that now. I would forever be indistinguishable from all the others who had not been chosen. I was just one of five hundred. One of five hundred million. I am the *addressee*, I kept thinking as the valedictorian droned on. I will always be the addressee.

I turned nineteen working at the restaurant, making $4.50 an hour. I turned twenty at $4.75. And twenty-one at $5.75. "This is just a stopping-through place," a busboy had told me on the day he quit. He was eighteen, blond hair, blue eyes, movie-star handsome with a dimple in his chin. He spoke with the expertise of someone who had done nothing to earn that expertise. I wanted to ask him for advice anyway. Instead I said, "You got that right, man," as if I were also an expert on the subject of life's trajectory. For my twenty-fifth birthday ($7.50), the waitresses got everyone to chip in to surprise me with a cake. "Happy birthday, Ike!" they sang at the end of the night. The twenty-five candles overwhelmed the cake. The flame was wide and significant; I saw the substance of my age. People joked about the restaurant catching fire. The waitresses had wanted to be nice, but I could see only pity. Who wants to celebrate his twenty-fifth birthday at an employees' table next to a mop closet while wearing a splattered apron and a checkered cook's uniform? I ate the cake to show my gratitude. My manager came by and slapped me on the back. "Congratulations," he said. He was the only person there who was older than I. The slap had a proprietary quality.

When I was about eighteen, a guy I knew from the neighborhood had seen me walking down the street and picked me up in his taxi. I was a block from home, but he wanted to drive me around and show off his new job. I sat in the backseat like a passenger, and I stared at the back of his head. "I'm celebrating my twenty-fifth birthday next week," he told me. "Big party. Come on by."

"Okay," I said.

"A quarter of a century," he said. He was being boastful, but the phrase was jarring. I can tell you this much, I wanted to say. When I'm a quarter of a century, I won't be driving any taxi.

I had dreams of grandeur. I didn't know how to get there, but I knew that it would work out.

He drove me around for a while and then he dropped me off right where we'd begun, a block from my house.

"See you at the party," he told me. But I didn't go.

I start at five o'clock and I stop at midnight. On weekends I stop at one o'clock. Sundays the restaurant is closed. Thursdays I have off. On busy nights, the dinner rush begins around seven and goes until eleven. There is relative calm in the kitchen at first, and then the sounds begin to take on a discernible urgency—voices, dishes, doors, not unlike light rain before heavy rain—and then there will be an explosion of orders. How is it possible? All these orders? All these orders at once? Oh my God! There are only three cooks and a salad guy, but there are fifty orders, and then there are a hundred orders. The white blur of the manager's shirt mixes with the black blurs of the waitresses'. Each cook in a pristine apron, soon to become filthy, hunches over a little workstation, cutting, frying, wiping, responsible for his little world. Once in a while, one cook will come to the aid of another who has fallen far behind, as if in battle, and this is always viewed as an act of extreme kindness. Generally, though, it's every man for himself, and we let one another die facedown in the mud. I move at a steady pace somewhere between frantic and perilous. Once I scalded my entire forearm with boiling water, but I wrapped the wound with cold towels and continued marching onward up the hill. Another time I lacerated the tip of my finger, and only after my shift was over did I go to the hospital for seven stitches. I have learned precision and efficiency over the years. There is no wasted motion in anything I do. I am a study of that thin line between human and machine. The order comes in, the eyes scan the order, one hand removes two slices of rye bread (for instance) and places the bread on the grill, the other hand is already reaching for the American cheese that is in the square tin on the shelf, while another order comes in and the eyes are scanning that order as the limbs and hands continue to move. Only when the rush begins to abate do I understand that I have been in something akin to a trance, moving constantly but without full consciousness. The sounds in the kitchen will get quieter, a gentle, nonessential clattering. A lullaby of clattering—it's near midnight, after all. The waitresses stand around idly. The dishwasher smokes a cigarette, even though he's not supposed to smoke in here. Afterward I walk the ten blocks to my apartment, and if I make it home in time, I watch the end of David Letterman.

A few days after I was turned down for a raise, an anorexic waitress started working at the restaurant. She was pretty but had no breasts or ass. I caught her a few times eating the scraps from customers' plates. She chewed and swallowed slowly, methodically, as if it took all her concentration. The waitresses said that they heard her sometimes in the bathroom coughing violently, and if they entered after her, they noticed traces of blood in the toilet.

The first time I saw her, she was sitting at the employees' table before the dinner shift, clipping flowers and placing them in vases. She looked up when I passed by, and I saw that her eyes were bright blue, contrasting with her hair, which was jet black. Her arms were thin and her shoulder blades protruded at a sharp angle. When our eyes met, she looked down quickly and then looked back up, and when she looked up, I looked away. A couple of days later, she was standing at the time clock trying to figure out how to punch out after her shift. I was just arriving at the restaurant, and my shoes were wet from the rain. "Here," I said. "Like this. You do it like this." I put her time card in and jiggled it, because sometimes it has to be jiggled, and the clock crunched out the time: 4:52 P.M. "What a piece of shit," she said. "The manager should fix that." Her voice was deep, considering how fragile she appeared. I saw that she had a red rash on her neck that she was trying to conceal with makeup. The rash seemed to be either creeping up toward her face or down onto her body, as if it might be the thing that had eaten away her breasts and her ass. Her elbow touched my elbow, but I couldn't tell if it was on purpose. And then my manager came into the break room.

"Busy night ahead of us," he said, and slapped me on the back.

"The time clock," the waitress said to him. "It doesn't work."

"Oh?" the manager said. He looked embarrassed. "I'll tell the fix-it guy."

He was wrong: it was a slow night. Which can be worse, because then one must make oneself busy. Or at least appear busy. A self-imposed punishment for the lack of business, as if the employees were to blame.

I spent my time polishing all the stainless steel in the kitchen, using an old jar of cream that guaranteed immediate results. It lived up to its billing, and I got satisfaction from seeing things gleam. When an order came in, it was burdensome, and I had to drag myself to the grill to put together whatever it was that had been requested. Tonight, I was certain, was not the night to ask again for a raise. I commended myself on my foresight. Occasionally I would look through the little round porthole of the kitchen door and see the anorexic waitress carrying trays of coffee mugs from one end of the restaurant to the other. How was it possible for her to carry a tray of coffee mugs? How was it possible for her to stand on those skinny legs? But she showed no signs of exertion in anything she did, like one of those small birds that take off with great power, beating their wings angrily. I should ask her out, I thought. We could come back here to eat. Take a long time looking at the menu. Inconvenience other people for a change. At the end we could ask to see the manager, and if he were feeling generous, he could waive the bill.

That night I sat on my couch and watched David Letterman interview a starlet. She wore unusually long earrings, high heels, and a red dress that I kept hoping I'd be able to see up. "What's your dream vacation?" Letterman asked her. "Oh, I just want to stay home in my pajamas," the starlet said. And David Letterman looked at the camera in that way he has, and everyone in the audience laughed, and Paul Shaffer played something quick on the keyboard, and the rain was coming down outside my window, and I realized that, shockingly, it was the anorexic waitress being interviewed by David Letterman. David Letterman was looking at the camera, which is to say he was looking at me, and he was saying, "Is it really that complicated for you to make a grilled cheese sandwich?" The anorexic waitress was holding a plate with a grilled cheese sandwich as evidence of my incompetence. "Why was this returned?" David Letterman was asking. But before I could respond the valedictorian said that some of us here tonight would either go into the military or enter directly into the workforce.

Suddenly I was wide awake on the couch. A police show was playing on the television. Buddy talk. I switched it off. Light was just beginning to break. I got up and paced around the living room and then I sat back down on the couch. The couch was soft; next to it was a chair and a lamp, all generously provided by the landlady. When I first came to look at the apartment, I was disconcerted to observe a refrigerator standing against the living room wall. "You can have that too," the landlady said, as if having a refrigerator in the living room were a desirable thing. I made a show of considering it. We walked out onto the balcony, which was the apartment's main selling point. It was a sunny day, and we stood together for a while, looking down five flights to the street. The previous tenant had spray-painted a pair of shoes on the balcony without bothering to put down newspaper as protection. Positioned between myself and the landlady was the permanent silhouette of two feet facing the railing. They had a ghostly quality, as if someone had leaped and left behind his imprint. I wanted to ask the landlady if she might be able to clean away those feet at some point, but I didn't ask and I took the apartment anyway.

Now I opened the balcony door and stood outside. It was raining lightly. Perhaps today was the day it would stop altogether. No one was out on the street. In the distance was a line of dense trees that in the dim light seemed closer than they actually were. Beyond the trees were the mountains. The mountains and the trees made the city seem rural, or on the verge of becoming rural, as if civilization were working in reverse and nature were reclaiming the land for itself. The mayor had countered this by referring to the city as "The Emerging International City." He hoped the moniker would catch on. So far it hadn't. On local television, there were commercials every fifteen minutes, poorly made, with people on the street pretending to make unprompted remarks about why the city was already an international city or deserved to be one. But it was clear that none of them really knew what they were talking about. Furthermore, the phrase "emerging international city" was so cumbersome and took such great concentration to say that you could detect, after watching these commercials over and over, the way people paused ever so slightly before uttering it. The very fact that everyone managed to pronounce the phrase without stumbling once was evidence that the whole man-on-the-street conceit was fraudulent.

Below my balcony, two black boys were riding by on bicycles. They were drenched from the rain and they were laughing and they were full of bravado. One of the boys happened to glance up at me. "What are you looking at, white man?" he yelled out, speeding away as if I might be able to swoop down and get him. I was humiliated, not by the use of "white" but by the use of "man." He sees me as a man, I thought. When I was eight years old, I had spent the afternoon playing with a group of my friends and a lone black boy who lived in the next neighborhood over. All afternoon we played, until another one of our friends showed up, making the lone black boy superfluous. "Time to go home, fella," my friend had told him. But the boy had refused to go home, and an argument ensued. My father heard the argument and threw open the kitchen window.

"Go home, boy," he said, assuming that the black boy was the cause of the trouble. "Go home before I come down there and slap the taste out of your mouth."

When I woke in the morning, it was raining hard. My downstairs neighbor hadn't taken in his newspaper yet, so I sat in the vestibule and read it.

Business is bad. That was the big news. Business is bad and the rain won't stop. Business is going to get better, but first it's going to get worse. The rain is going to get worse too. And then the rain will stop.

When my neighbor came down, he was wearing a gray bathrobe.

"Here's your paper," I said, as if I'd been standing in the vestibule with his newspaper in my hands for the purpose of handing it to him.

He looked aggrieved. "Thank you," he said. Hollow words. He folded the paper and put it under his arm; his armpit was stained. He nodded at me. "Have a great day," he said.

Later, I did my exercises. I do them every day. If I ever end up joining the military, I will be ready. But I have no intention of joining the military. A couple of years ago, on the basketball court, an older guy had come over after the game and talked to me about life. He was friendly and showed interest, and I thought he might be gay. He smiled at everything I said.

"Is that right, son?" At the end of our conversation, he handed me his business card: Sergeant Robert Alton. "Stop by, son, and talk to me sometime." I thought about stopping by, but what I really wanted was for him to come back to the basketball court and ask me again to stop by sometime.

I did fifty push-ups, straight and with no effort. Several minutes later I did fifty more. Those took effort. Then I did sit-ups. The room vibrated. When I was done, I examined my body in the mirror. Sharp corners met round corners. When I turned to the side, the sharpness gave way to roundness. The body of a hamster, I thought. And then I thought about the anorexic waitress standing next to me at the time clock. The body of a hamster meets the body of a bird. "Here," the hamster said. "Like this. You do it like this." And the bird's wing touched the hamster's paw, but it was not clear if this was intentional.

On Saturday night, I decided I would ask again for a raise. Especially considering that one of the other cooks had not shown up for his shift. I was covering for him, a near-impossibility, because that night the orders were unceasing. I loathed the waitresses who brought them to me, even the anorexic one. The manager said that he would come and help out, as if he had any idea what needed to be done, as if anyone could just drop in and do my job. But he didn't help, and I saw this as even more reason to ask for a raise. "I'm looking to move up to . . ." "I'm looking to move up from . . ."

Near midnight, things finally slowed down. My apron was splattered, as if I had been shot with food the way people are sometimes shot with paint for fun. The dishwasher smoked a cigarette, and I hoped the manager would come in and catch him. Through the window of the kitchen door, I could see the anorexic waitress tallying up her tips for the night. The way she concentrated over the pile of money accentuated her cheekbones. I knew she'd be gone by the time I was done cleaning up my workstation. A last-second order came in, and I got it ready. And then I scrubbed the grill with a long wire brush. I was supposed to scrub it every night, but I never did, and no one noticed. Tonight, though, there would be no evidence that could be used against me. Hard bits of ash that had accumulated over the years fell from the grates like ants. My shoulder ached from the exertion. When I looked through the window, sure enough, the anorexic waitress was gone.

Just a few more odds and ends to finish up, I thought, but when I turned around, my manager was standing there with a plate in his hand. "What's this?" he asked.

On the plate was a grilled cheese sandwich: the bread was almost black, but the cheese, as my manager showed me, had not melted.

"How do you burn the bread, Ike," he asked, "but not melt the cheese?" His face was kind.

Outside, I stood under the restaurant awning. The rain was coming down in great sheets. The wind and the dark gave it the quality of a volcanic eruption. People were saying that this was it—the final rainfall—and that as early as tomorrow morning or tomorrow afternoon it was going to be sunny. They'd heard this said.

I started walking. My umbrella was no defense. After two blocks, the black fabric tore away beneath the onslaught, so that I was holding only the sagging frame of an umbrella. Why could no umbrella be invented to withstand a downpour? When I was sixteen years old, I had filled out an application at school for a summer job and then forgotten about it until I was called one June morning to meet with the supervisor of an umbrella factory. It was a small family-owned place on the outskirts of town, where some factories still existed. I had to take three buses to get there. The supervisor was a perspiring man in a tie and a shirt with one button missing from the center. He was looking for an office clerk. He asked what my skills were, but I didn't know what they were, because I'd never had a job. I told him I was a hard worker, because I assumed that this would be true if I was given the opportunity, and he seemed to accept it at face value. Afterward, he showed me around the plant. It was old and made of wood, and there were probably mice. A group of ex-farmers, or people who looked like they might be ex-farmers, stood around a long table spray-painting assorted logos onto umbrellas. I was curious about their work, and the supervisor took me closer so I could see. The smell of paint was pleasant and reminded me of my kindergarten days. "It smells great," I said to the supervisor, grinning. He looked askance at me, and within thirty seconds the smell had become so overwhelming, so noxious, that I feared I might vomit. "Let's get away from these characters," the supervisor said. He showed me the office where I would be working. It had a file cabinet and a swivel chair and a window that looked out onto the factory floor. I pictured myself sitting at the desk and wearing a tie, and the image invigorated me. Two days later, the supervisor called to offer me the job, and I told him it was too far away for me, but I thanked him anyway.

Three blocks from my apartment, I could see that I had left the lamp on in the living room. In the dark, it looked like a beacon of sorts. The hair on half of my head was matted from the rain. A car approached from the opposite direction, spraying water on both sides. It steered toward me, and for a moment I thought that it might be some punks looking to drive through a puddle and splash me. Then it slowed and stopped completely, and the window came down and the anorexic waitress leaned her head out. "Get in, silly," she said.

There was another girl in the car, so I got in the backseat.

"I just live right there," I said, pointing, but instead of turning the car around, she drove over the bridge, past the railroad tracks, up into the hills.

"This is my friend," the anorexic waitress said, looking at me in the rearview mirror, but the windshield wipers were clacking and I couldn't catch the friend's name.

She was in college, this friend. Or about to go to college. The anorexic waitress was going to the same college in the spring. I couldn't hear what she planned to study. She spoke as if she were already weary of it. Her thin hands gripped the steering wheel. In her black waitress blouse, her arms looked the diameter of fingers. Could those even be called arms? But she drove with ferocity. Up into the hills we went, those dark hills that looked as if they were encroaching on the city. Shortly we were in the thick of them, and I was surprised to discover that, rather than being the heart of the rural world, they were the heart of the suburbs. Nice houses that looked identical were set catercorner to one another off the main road. Billboards directed us to more houses about to be built, and to a mall I'd been hearing about for a while. Another billboard showed an illustration of a spinning earth with an arrow pointing to a small dot that presumably was where we were. THE EMERGING INTERNATIONAL CITY, it read.

Soon we were dropping the friend off in front of her parents' large house. The house was dark except for one light that illuminated the driveway. "Good night! Good night!" she called.

I took the front seat and I noticed how wet my pants were. I noticed how close I was to the anorexic waitress. Back toward the city we went. In the gloomy swirl of rain, I could see the giant office building with its antenna that, in the darkness, looked like a cross on a church steeple.

"Do you want to hear a riddle?" she asked out of the blue.

"Okay," I said.

She smiled broadly. Her teeth looked discolored. "There's a cabin in the woods with two dead people. They are both strapped to chairs." She paused to glance my way. "The doors of the cabin are blocked and the windows are sealed. The people did not die from murder, exposure, dehydration, suicide, fire, asphyxiation, disease, or starvation. What did they die from?"

She concentrated as if she were also trying to think of the answer. I thought about the word "starvation." I had no idea what the answer was, so I guessed AIDS.

No.

I guessed again.

No.

"Should we really be talking about dying while you're driving in the rain?" I asked. She let out a ghoulish movie laugh and pantomimed turning the wheel hard, as if to swerve into oncoming traffic. This made me tense. The windshield wipers beat out their rhythm. "What killed them?" she said again. We went around a bend, and the office building disappeared momentarily and then reappeared, so that its giant antenna resembled a needle stuck in an arm.

"It's an airplane, silly," she said. "They're seat-belted into the *cabin* of an airplane that's crashed in the woods."

I thought about this, piecing it back together from the opposite end. "That's a good riddle," I said at last.

"I know," she said. "I've got a lot of them."

We were coming back over the railroad tracks that were about a mile from my apartment. A dishwasher from the restaurant once managed to elude the police who had come to arrest him in the middle of his shift, and not knowing where to go, he had run all the way to the tracks and hidden in the underbrush. They'd found him three hours later, covered in dirt, and taken him to jail. At his trial, he had pleaded no contest on the advice of his court-appointed lawyer so that he'd get only a three-year sentence. He had not known what the phrase meant, though, and so, standing in the courtroom in his baggy suit, he had said, "No *contents*," and everyone in the courtroom had laughed.

"What are you thinking about?" she asked me abruptly. "What are you so quiet for?"

I told her about the dishwasher, and she said, "That's a funny story." And then she said, "That's a strange story."

After that she said she had thought about studying law but decided against it. But might study it after all.

"You're a funny boy," she said. "You know that?" And it was my turn to smile, because it'd been a long time since any-one had called me a boy. When had I crossed that line from boy to man? Whenever it was, the line had been so faint, so subtle, that I had missed it entirely. Maybe if I had been pay-ing closer attention, things might have turned out differently for me.

" 'Boy,' " I said. "That's a weird thing to call me."

So she said it again. "Boy . . . boy . . . boy." Teasing now. But suddenly she was no longer saying just "boy" but "pretty boy." Or perhaps I had misheard her. "Pretty boy." I wanted to ask if I was hearing her correctly, because the rain was loud, and the car was loud, and she was driving with great vigor along the wet streets, all the power of her skeletal limbs surg-ing into the car. I watched her mouth, waiting for it to speak again. A wide mouth with wide lips. Her lips were the fleshiest part of her body. The second I looked back toward the street, I heard her say it again.

"Pretty boy," she said. "Pretty, pretty boy."

"Really?" I asked her. "Really?"

ASSOCIATES

It was about a month after the war began that I took two boxes off the Walmart truck and hid them in the mop closet. I wasn't proud of my behavior, considering I'm the assistant manager, but I was in love with a girl who might or might not have been in love with me. Either way, this was the necessary course of action.

When the truck pulled up to the loading dock, I opened it myself and walked around being a pest with my clipboard, punctilious and official, examining things, checking things off my list. The driver kept sighing and coughing and making all manner of frustrated sounds. "It takes as long as it takes," I said. Finally he went to piss, and while he was away, I grabbed the boxes and fled to the mop closet. I took a big box of toilet paper, sixty-two count, and I took a big box of something else that I didn't bother to look at. I just grabbed it. Cookies or cupcakes, I think it was. It didn't matter. I didn't care. Mr. Bildman didn't care either. He took whatever you brought him. He took motor oil. He took nail polish remover. He took apples and oranges.

About an hour later, I tracked down Joey Joey in the break room, talking to three cashiers. He had his feet up on the chair like he owned the place, like an asshole. When he saw me, he stood up and saluted. The girls laughed. Jenna and Haley and Lisa Marie. He was putting on a show for them.

"I'm going to need your help with something," I said.

"You got it, cap'n!" he said.

He calls me "cap'n" all the time and I'm not sure what he intends by it other than to irritate or possibly humiliate me. When he isn't calling me "cap'n," he's calling me "sarge" or "colonel." It might have been tolerable if there'd been some trace of irony in his voice. We're friends, after all, we grew up together, we played Little League together, we graduated from high school together. But I've been promoted three times and he's remained an associate. "You know why, right?" he said once. "It's because you're good-looking." No, it's because I'm more diligent than he, more industrious, and somewhat more intelligent. It's also because while I was working my way up at Walmart—beginning with cleaning the bathrooms—he was selling prescription drugs, dressing as if every night was prom night, carrying a roll of money the size of a baseball, and driving around the city in an SUV with ROAD TO THE RICHES hand-lettered on the side. He was sure that this was it, that he had found his calling and the good times would never end. But the good times ended when he got arrested and the fear of God was put in him. I went to visit him twice at the county jail with Chip, who also went all the way back to Little League. A window with fingerprints separated us and we had to talk over a telephone, Chip and I taking turns. There was a disconcerting hitch in the mechanism so that Joey Joey's lips moved before I heard the words in the receiver. It was like I was watching a movie that had been dubbed in English. He was wearing a baggy green shirt and an ID bracelet, and if you didn't know any better, you would have thought he was a patient in a hospital, which I guess in some ways he was. He had a small bruise on the side of his head, and when I asked him how he had come by it, he told me he'd dropped a dumbbell lifting weights. It was a story I found hard to believe, since he'd never worked out in his life. He spoke at length about his innocence, about how it was all a misunderstanding. He was facing six to eight years, but he managed to affect an assertive, nonchalant voice, highly enunciated designed to persuade the authorities who were presumed to be listening in on the conversation (which may have accounted for the delay on the telephone). But his eyes were the opposite of confident; they were wide, white, and tense. The next time Chip and I went to visit, the warden had locked down the jail and visiting hours were suspended. We left Joey Joey twenty dollars on his account, along with a porno magazine. Not long after, he went to court with a decent lawyer and pleaded no contest to a misdemeanor. He ended up serving eight months. Ever since then he's had some catching up to do.

At six o'clock I left the store with my spreadsheets and a cup of coffee. "See you tomorrow, Mr. McDonough," the cashiers called out sycophantically.

A long line of customers was filing in with their shopping

carts and their babies and I had to jostle my way to get through. It was chilly outside but getting warmer day by day. It had been a rough winter and now we were hoping for a nice spring. The clocks had just been set ahead and the sunshine was pleasant but disconcerting. It made me feel like the last ten hours spent indoors had been doubly squandered. I drove my car around to the back where the garbage dumpsters stood in a row. No one was around. No one had any business being around. I turned on the radio and drank my coffee and listened to some news about baseball and about the war. I shut it off. Sitting in the silent cocoon of the car, with the sun beginning to go down, familiar fatigue came over me, originating in the soles of my feet and emanating upward until I felt soft and heavy. Even the coffee couldn't offset the effects. It was warm in the car and I turned on the AC and it blew in my face. I took out my BlackBerry and checked my email. I have a tendency to check my email compulsively, especially when I'm idle. There were four new emails, all from work, all forwarded by people who had cc'd fifty people. It was what you did when you were trying to get out of responsibility, when you wanted to pass the buck to the next guy—you cc'd everyone. "Accounts Payable Protocol" was the subject line of one. I didn't bother to read any of them.

In my lap lay my spreadsheets, rows and columns of blocks, some of those blocks filled, some of them empty; by tomorrow morning they'd all be filled in by me. They looked like a road map of sorts, my spreadsheets, an aerial view of the city, little block by little block, and I considered the drive I was about to make to Winchester Parks and whether I should take the expressway or the bridge. I thought about Mr. Bildman, and I thought about Mr. Bildman's daughter, Zlottie. She liked me, but I wasn't sure if she liked me as *more than just a friend*. A slight tremble of anxiety passed through me, briefly counterbalancing the fatigue. It had been a while since I'd had a girlfriend, a real girlfriend, mainly because I was shy, but also because I worked all the time and I couldn't find any girls I liked. But Zlottie was smart, she was also sophisticated, and she had the darkest eyes. She had the darkest hair too. In short, she was the most beautiful girl I'd ever met.

The last time I'd seen her was right before Christmas. I'd gone to the shop with Chip. Chip had the connection and I had the car. He'd brought with him sixteen boxes of underpants that he'd taken off the truck at Kmart. "I don't give a fuck," he said. He'd been at Kmart seven years and was about to deploy and had nothing left to lose. He'd lost it all already when he blew out his knee senior year and his basketball scholarship was revoked. He'd shown me the letter the college sent him upon hearing the news, a giant coat of arms telling him they'd be happy to still have him if he could come up with twenty-five thousand dollars a year. He was six-foot-six but walked with a slouch, all shoulders, no neck, as if trying to get back to normal height so he could forget the whole thing. Instead of going to college, he'd signed up for the reserves. When he'd gotten called up, I'd told him, "You'll be back before you know it." I'd been one of those fools who thought there wasn't even going to be a war. Now that's exactly where he was.

When we'd walked into Mr. Bildman's shop that final day, Zlottie had been right in the front, standing on a ladder stacking boxes of crackers. On the shelf behind her was one of those Jewish candelabras with half the candles lit. The shop glowed in a soft light, making Zlottie look dramatic on the ladder, like an angel descending. She was wearing the same thing she always wore: a long black skirt that dropped all the way down to her shoes like a curtain on a stage and which hid the good parts from view. Even so, I could make out the curve of her ass. While Chip was in the back sorting out the details with Mr. Bildman, I broke the news that I wouldn't be coming back. It was Chip's thing, after all, and I was only the driver, and he was going off to war—and I wasn't really a thief.

"That's that," I said. I tried to sound detached.

"Okay," she said.

She didn't seem to be affected by it that much. Apparently I was the only one with feelings. It was dark enough in the store that Zlottie, in her dark outfit, was almost beginning to disappear before my eyes. Then she caught me by surprise by saying, "Well, I'm just glad it's not you shipping out, Nick." Her voice sounded poignant in a time of war.

Since then I'd masturbated every day, sometimes twice a day, thinking about her working in that dusty shop, with that long black hair and that long black skirt, me entering with a box of whatnot, and the candles lit romantically.

From around the corner of the loading dock, Joey Joey appeared, pushing a big green dumpster that said WALMART on the side. He looked lethargic. His blue shirt was half untucked and there was sweat under the armpits. His pale face and round head added to the quality of lethargy.

"Oooooh," he said as I rolled down the window. "I don't

think this is a good idea, Nick." The teenage humor from earlier was gone. Outside the walls of Walmart, he was all sniffles
and submission. That's what jail had done to him. Eight years
in the penitentiary would have turned him into a rabid, raging
fiend, but eight months in county jail had sapped his spirit. I
felt a pang of remorse for having recruited him in a crime that
was for my benefit only. "I'll make this worth your while," I
said.

I got out of the car, and together we pulled my big box of
toilet paper and my other big box out of the dumpster. There
was slime on the boxes, grease or something, but they were no
worse for the wear. Mr. Bildman would take them.

I chose wrong and took the expressway. It was bumper-to-
bumper. Joey Joey passed the time by flipping back and forth
through my spreadsheets. I checked my email. It was getting
dark out, and my BlackBerry glowed with emails of cc's. Every
few seconds we'd crawl a foot and then stop. All the cars had
flags on them, or red-white-and-blue bumper stickers, or some
indication that we were in the midst. Occasionally someone
would yell out a car window. "Niiiiiiiiiiiiiiiick!" they'd yell, or
"Joey JoEYYYYYYYYY!" because we'd lived in this city all
our lives and we knew everyone.

"I could do this," Joey Joey said, meaning my spreadsheets, meaning my job.

"Why don't you, then?" I said.

He guffawed. Then he got quiet while he pondered.
"Twenty," he said, "thirty-three, one-oh-seven." He pointed
with schoolboy pride at the little empty city blocks on the
spreadsheet.

"Oh yeah?" I said. "What about the weekend?"

He pondered again. He tallied on his fingers. "Twenty-nine," he announced, "thirty-four, two-eleven."

He was right, he probably could do my job. But he wouldn't. He'd just talk about doing it. He didn't have that *thing* anymore, whatever that *thing* was that got you ahead in life. He'd fallen hard and couldn't get back up. Maybe he'd never really had that *thing*. Maybe he was the kind of person who was better at taking orders than giving them. "That boy moves like a coon," my father once said. He was a boorish man, my father, unschooled and unskilled, pretty much like the rest of the people in my neighborhood. I'm the one who ended up accomplishing something, making something of myself, and now I had to live with everyone thinking that they could do my job, that what I've earned is because of some secret to which they don't have access: ill-gotten gains. The real secret is I worked sixty hours last week, not including the work I took home. The week before I worked seventy. I get full benefits and three weeks' vacation, but I've done the math, and when it's all added up, my salary isn't much above minimum wage. About the only thing that separates me from the associates is that I wear a white shirt instead of a blue one. Often I'll fantasize about when times were simple and I carried a box cutter and waited around for someone to tell me what to do. Other times I fantasize about moving up to upper management, which is at least ten years away if things go right. In ten years I'll be thirty-six. I'll have a potbelly and I'll be bald. I'll look like the district manager who drives a yellow Mercedes with a license plate that says WLMRT-1. He says to me, "I was just like you once, Nick." He wants to keep me motivated.

I got off at Exit 12 and circled back down and took the bridge. I was speeding, I didn't care, I was trying to make up for lost time. When I took the turn, Joey Joey had to put his hands on the dashboard. Down below, the river had a nice tint in the evening light, and on both sides of the river were the factories pumping out smoke for the war effort. Twenty-four hours a day, they pumped out smoke.

"I should get a job down there," Joey Joey said, tapping the window. He sounded wistful.

"You'd be back in a week," I said, "begging to be an associate again."

"Maybe, maybe not," he said. He was looking at the river. He was talking more to himself than me. "Might go ahead and join up," he said. "Might just do that."

I'd heard it before. He'd talked about it during the peace and during the buildup. He'd talked about it when the shooting first started. He'd be talking about it when everyone came home. He'd probably be talking about it during the next war. He didn't have that *thing*.

"Join up," he continued, "head over there, see Chip, have an adventure. Blow some people up." He snickered. "Get in shape." He pinched his muffin top by way of example. "Maybe, maybe not," he said.

At the top of the hill I made a left into Winchester Parks and then a right. It was called Winchester Parks but there wasn't anything green about it anymore. It'd been an Italian neighborhood, it'd been a Jewish neighborhood, now it was up for grabs. Way down at the end of the street, I could see the long row of stores, with Bildman's shop in the middle. It had a red neon sign that was lit up: BILDMANS SH P. On one side of the shop was a pizza place and on the other was a Chinese store that sold remedies. I slowed down because I was suddenly nervous about seeing Zlottie, suddenly unprepared, suddenly didn't know what I was doing or why exactly I'd come. "I thought you said you weren't coming anymore," she'd say. She'd be confused. I'd be embarrassed.

At the stop sign, I took a long time. Out in front of Mr. Bildman's shop were boxes filled with little American flags being sold for ninety-nine cents each. The pizza place had a sign saying that if you were a soldier, you could get a slice for half price. "I should tell them I'm a marine," Joey Joey said.

I pulled over and checked my face in the rearview mirror. I checked my teeth and I checked my email. I leaned over and popped the glove compartment and took out a tin of Altoids. There were five tins of Altoids in the glove compartment. I'd bought them at Walmart. Almost everything I owned I'd bought at Walmart: toothpaste, socks, you name it. Walmart helped keep me alive and I helped keep them in business. I put three Altoids in my mouth.

"Can I have one?" Joey Joey said.

I gave him a whole tin. "Wait here," I said.

The door jingled when I entered the shop. I was anticipating seeing Zlottie on the ladder, the way she had appeared in my late-night and early-morning fantasies. Instead, I saw her father. He was standing behind the counter with a handful of slips of green paper. His black hat was on the counter and his head was bald. He was wearing his black wash-and-wear suit that he wore every day. His enormous white beard seemed to have grown more enormous since the last time I'd seen him, more cloud than beard. It looked untrimmed and unwashed.

The shop looked unwashed. It was small and cramped, about the size of the customer bathroom at Walmart, and it was loaded floor to ceiling with anything you might ever need in life. I'd once seen a boy come in and ask for a can of sardines and a pack of baseball cards, and Mr. Bildman had them bagged and ready to go in under a minute.

At some point we'd swallow this shop whole. I'd be the district manager by then and this would be my district. That would be an example of irony.

Mr. Bildman looked up from his green slips. He didn't seem particularly happy to see me. I stood in the center of the store holding my boxes of merchandise like one of those trainers who showcases a dog at the tournament. I hoped he liked my boxes.

"Put them in the back," he said.

I wanted to ask him where his daughter was, because if his daughter wasn't there, I wasn't interested. But I went dutifully to the back room. There was a gunmetal desk standing like an island amid towers of more odds and ends. I set the boxes on the desk and sat down in the swivel chair and waited. I was prepared for something to fall on my head. I checked my BlackBerry. Now and then I would hear the door jangle and I would listen for Zlottie's voice but it was always a customer. Every customer wanted some kind of break. "I'll pay you the rest next week," they all said.

I started to wonder if Zlottie had taken off, moved or something, gone to Israel. She'd talked about Israel the way old people I knew talked about Ireland. She'd also talked about going back to school. We'd had heartfelt discussions while I was waiting around for Chip to get his money. She would stand on the opposite side of the counter with the cash register, but it felt close, like the counter was a part of us and we were pressing our bodies against it as we stood staring at each other. She was the only person who ever asked me what my plans were for the future, and I'd tell her about becoming a district manager. "Wow," she'd say, "that's exciting, Nick." It sounded like she was sincere, but who knows. I always made a point of encouraging her to get her degree, because I wanted her to see that I was one of those kind of people who could be optimistic and helpful. Now I regretted it. I should have encouraged her to remain in the shop forever.

Mr. Bildman came into the back office. He didn't look at the boxes I'd brought, he just said, "I'll give you sixty for everything."

It was a generous figure, far more than I'd thought it would be. It made me wonder if Chip had been duplicitous when he'd hand me fifteen bucks on the way home and tell me it was half.

"I'll take it," I said.

He had it right there in his pocket. He handed it to me. He wanted me out of the shop as fast as possible, as if he knew what I'd really come for. He was one of those fathers who didn't want anyone to lay a finger on his daughter. I stood up and he sat down.

"Tell Zlottie I said hi," I said.

He snapped his head sharply. "What?"

I repeated myself. He nodded. He wasn't going to tell her a thing.

But as I came out of the back office, there she was, just like that, like a vision, standing on the top rung of the ladder stacking cans of soup. Here was my fantasy come alive. She was wearing the same black skirt with the same black shoes, and her hair was as black as I remembered. She must have thought I was her father, because she said something like "I'm almost done," and then she accidentally dropped a can of soup. It banged and rolled. I bent down to retrieve it, and when I looked up, she was staring at me with surprise. I could feel my face burn red, and the heat from my face traveled straight down my body.

"What are you doing here, Nick?" she said. She laughed, as if my appearance was comical. This wasn't what I had fantasized. I stood there staring at her. She hovered above me in the air, five rungs high on the ladder, the shelves of merchandise floating behind her head.

"I missed you, Zlottie," I said. I wanted it to come out breezy, but it sounded earnest and maybe a little pathetic.

I handed her the can of soup. She reached for it and her skirt rode up an inch past her ankle.

"I missed you too," she said, but she grinned so broadly that I couldn't tell whether she was teasing or not.

And then the door tinkled, and I heard someone saying, "Nick, hey. Hey, Nick. About how much longer you think you're going to be here?" Joey Joey stood in the doorway with a slice of pizza.

"You know why you don't get ahead?" I said to him. "It's because you don't know how to follow orders."

"Awwwwww," Zlottie said. "That's not nice." But before I could explain to her what kind of person Joey Joey was, and what kind of person I was, and how he never listened, and how I was a hard worker, something like six customers came charging through the front door and our moment was lost for-ever. She didn't even say goodbye.

On the drive home, I gave Joey Joey fifteen dollars. He took some cash out of his pocket, which he still carried in a roll like the old days, and which looked to be about twenty-five dollars, and he carefully folded my fifteen dollars into it. I waited for him to say thank you.

After a while, he said, "You know that hair isn't real."

"What's that?" I said.

"The Jewgirl," he said, "she's wearing a wig."

We were coming over the bridge now, it was night and the river was illuminated by the factories. We'd gone fishing down in that river, this is years ago, me, Joey Joey, Chip. Before the factories opened back up, the river had fish. For five hours we fished, but we didn't catch a thing. It wasn't until there was about thirty minutes of daylight left that Chip's line drew taut. "I got something!" he screamed. The line got so tight that we had to help him hang on. Fishermen came and gave us advice. "It's going to be seaweed," they guessed. "It's going to be a tire." No, it was a turtle hanging from the end of the line, spinning in the air like a top, waving its legs. Chip took it home and kept it as a pet, named it Zero and painted its shell purple. It lived six years, and when it died we went back down to the river to bury it, but by then the factories had opened and you couldn't get within five hundred feet of the shore.

"I'm not thinking about any Jewgirl," I said.

But it wasn't a week later that I took three more boxes off the Walmart truck and hid them in the mop closet.

I found Joey Joey in the break room with his feet up.

"I'm going to need your help with something," I said.

"You got it, sarge!"

At six o'clock, the cashiers called out on cue, "See you tomorrow, Mr. McDonough."

I walked through the oncoming surge of customers and straight into a group of college students who make it a point to come by every Friday evening to cause problems. They were walking around in a circle, twenty or so, looking sentimental and holding signs with a long list of goals for Walmart, which, if ever achieved, would cost me my job. I had to walk through them like a gauntlet. I didn't appreciate that. One of the guys held out a flyer.

"If you want respect, give respect," I said.

He must have misunderstood my allegiance, because he laughed. "You got that right, bro."

"I ain't your bro," I said.

Now he was confused and conferred with the others. I passed through them.

"Overrated businessman," one of the girls yelled after me, but the comment had not been uttered with consensus. I could hear them begin to argue.

"We're all bros," half of them said.

"No, we're not," the other half countered.

No, yes, no.

Back by the dumpsters, I sat in my car. I'd just worked eleven hours and the exhaustion came over me like a wave. Slowly I changed out of my white shirt and into a new blue one from a three-pack I'd bought that morning. I wanted

Zlottie to see me in something other than a white shirt when I asked her out. Just like I wanted to see her in something other than a black skirt. Looking at myself in the rearview mirror, I was surprised to find a much younger version of myself looking back, a self from when I was an associate and wore a blue shirt almost the same color as the one I had on now. My younger version was good-looking and optimistic, and he walked briskly up and down the aisles looking for the assistant manager to tell him what it was he should do next.

"Mr. McDonough," I addressed myself in the reflection of the rearview mirror, "what do you want me to do next?"

"This is what you do next, Nick," myself answered, "you take these three boxes off the truck and then you hide them in the mop closet and then you go find Joey Joey . . ."

I woke to the sound of Joey Joey tapping on the window. His pale face was an inch from mine, separated only by the glass, like I was back visiting him in jail, except this time his mouth was wide with mirth. I rolled down the window.

"You were drooling, Nick," he said. He let out a howl. Sure enough, there was a wet stain on my blue shirt.

"Open the dumpster, jackass," I commanded. I was in no mood.

The boxes were large and hard to fit in the trunk. Since he'd blown my moment last time with Zlottie, I handed him five dollars and told him I'd see him tomorrow.

"I don't mind coming," he said. I left him standing there by the dumpster, his blue shirt half-untucked.

I drove fast and I took the bridge and I practiced what I would say. I would try to be casual, but also charming, and I would lean on the counter with my elbows as if it were no big deal to say, "I've got Tuesday off, Zlottie, and I was wondering . . ."

"I've got the Thursday after next off, Zlottie . . ."

"I've got a Sunday at the end of the month . . ."

In less than twenty minutes I was coming around the bend into Winchester Parks. This time I didn't linger at the stop sign but drove straight to the front of the store and parked. Once there, I procrastinated badly. I checked my email twice. I checked my face and my blue shirt. I checked my teeth. From the glove compartment, I took out three Altoids, put them in my mouth, and chewed them like candy. I checked my email again. Something had arrived, but it was from an unfamiliar address with a distressing subject line that read, "Not dead yet," and which I thought must be spam until I opened it and saw that it was a message from Chip.

"Dear Nick," he wrote, "I finally got my personal pfc. military account set up. They sure do have every thing down here. . . ." He went on to list the Internet café where he was writing from at that very moment, some fast-food places, and some other necessary hometown conveniences including a shoeshine stand, even though he'd never used a shoeshine stand in his life. He said things weren't so bad overall. It was boring mostly. More boring than he thought it would be. It was colder too. He was hoping for some new gloves to come through. And some boots, size fourteen. Other than that, everything was fine. He had no real complaints. It was like being in the Boy Scouts, he said. He was hoping to see a little action soon so he could kick some ass and break up the monotony, but he wasn't counting on it. He told me not to believe what I was hearing on the news. He said everything was exaggerated. He said it was all about advertising. In closing, he wanted to know how I was.

There was a time difference of some twelve hours, whether forward or backward I couldn't tell, but as far as I could see, he'd sent the message a few minutes earlier. Hoping that I might have a chance to catch him before he logged out, I quickly wrote,

Does your army base have a Kmart?
Your friend,
Nick

Before I could click send, however, I had a second thought that this might come across more mean-spirited than witty, so I backspaced over it.

In its place, I composed something delicate and thoughtful, how at the very moment I was sitting in Winchester Parks with three boxes of Walmart merchandise in my trunk about to ask Mr. Bildman's daughter out on a date, he, Chip, was sitting in an Internet café on the other side of the world. "By the way," I asked, "were you being up-front on how much Mr. Bildman was paying you for the boxes?"

Then I had the thought that this question was too trivial, given what he was going through, even if he wasn't going through much, so I backspaced over that, too. Then I backspaced over everything because he might not want to hear me crooning about Mr. Bildman's daughter and philosophizing about the speed of the Internet, while I sat in the comfort of my car and he waited for some new boots that fit his feet.

After that, I sat there staring at my blank BlackBerry not knowing what to write to him, wishing quite frankly that he'd never sent me anything at all, wishing that I could ignore the email altogether. Now I was the one stuck having to picture things that were unpleasant about my friend, like him sitting in the Internet café, his enormous frame slouching in the chair, typing away to his mom, to his girlfriend, to me, probably saying pretty much the same thing to each of us, hoping that someone would write back before his fifteen minutes of allotted time expired.

So I wrote,

> Kick some ass!
> Your friend,
> Nick

I clicked send fast and got out of my car. I opened my trunk and the butterflies returned. The boxes were big and unwieldy, bottles of laundry detergent and the like, and I regretted not having brought Joey Joey along to help. I teetered under their weight. I hoped Zlottie would not notice me teetering.

But when I got to the front door, I saw that the lights were off and there was a sign taped to the window. CLOSED FOR SHABBOS.

So I had to wait. I had to wait four days until my day off. On my days off, I usually sleep till noon, but I was awake at seven, thinking about what to wear. I ended up putting on a suit and tie. Dark suit, white shirt, dark tie. I thought it'd be good for her to see me in professional attire. "You look like a senator, Nick," she'd say. I took the tie off—business casual. "Oh, this is just what I wear when I'm not working," I'd say. Then I took everything off and masturbated.

When I got to the store, I had to get the big boxes out of the trunk again. All the pushing and pulling wrinkled my clothes and pissed me off. The door jingled like a sleigh bell when I entered, but Zlottie didn't hear me because three Chinese women were crowding the counter, screaming about some apples and oranges. They were sitting on top of the counter, the apples and oranges, and the Chinese women kept picking them up and putting them down as if this would prove their point. I couldn't see Zlottie, but I could hear her voice. "I'm sorry," she kept saying over and over. In the face of the customers' displeasure, she was as polite as ever, her voice as sweet as ever. "You, you, you," the women said, unswayed. They were short and round, and they wore polka-dot outfits that could have been pajamas. They crowded her like bullies. Somebody was trying to rip somebody off, and it wasn't clear whom. I could imagine Zlottie's father sitting at his gunmetal desk in the back room, oblivious to his daughter's dilemma.

The women must have thought I was an official in my suit, a detective maybe, because they got quiet and made way for me. "What seems to be the problem here?" I said. I set my boxes down on the counter, amid their apples and oranges, and I smiled at Zlottie, who, even in her distress, looked beautiful. Strands of black hair dangled in front of one eye.

"You, you, you," they said to Zlottie, but in my presence

the fight had gone out of them. They paid the ticket price and gathered their fruit and left. The door jingled three times.

In their wake, it was silent. In the silence, Zlottie blurted, "You, you, you," with breathy exaggeration, and she pulled the corners of her eyes so that they slanted. Her imitation was surprisingly good. I laughed. Then I took the high ground: "There's good and bad in all races," I said.

She thought about it. "That's true," she said.

It was something my father had told me in his better moments. "There's good and bad in all races, Nick." He had an obsession with good and bad, the latter of which generally included, among others, Jewish people. When I was about six years old, he had observed me peeling a banana without first washing it. "What's wrong with YOU?" he had shouted as if I were about to insert a burning torch into my mouth. He got off the couch and pounded his hands on his legs. His face was contorted with terror and fear, and this made me cry. "You see them in the supermarket putting their hands over everything!" Then calmly, patiently, lovingly, he said, "Go wash that banana in the sink, Nicholas."

"You look like a salesman, Nick," Zlottie said. I couldn't tell if this was a compliment.

"Thank you," I said.

"A door-to-door salesman," she continued. "What did you bring"—she patted my boxes—"encyclopedias?" She laughed. "Girl Scout cookies?"

"Zlottie," I said, leaning toward her and pressing hard against the counter and speaking too loudly. "I happen to have a Sunday off at the end of the month—"

But before I could finish she'd already said yes.

* * *

I'd been wrong about Joey Joey: maybe he did have that *thing*. Because when he came in to work the next day, he informed me that he had joined the army.

"Effective immediately, brigadier general!" he said. He saluted and clicked his heels.

Apparently he'd gone down to the Career Center, taken a physical, signed some papers, and now he was officially a soldier.

"I've got twenty-eight percent body fat," he said. "That's not too bad."

I told him I was proud of him and gave him the rest of the day off. In turn, he invited me over to his mom's house that weekend for a going-away party. Then he spent the rest of the afternoon walking around the store shaking hands with the guys and getting kissed by the girls. By the time he was done, he looked like his face had been painted with a Magic Marker.

It was eight P.M. when I left the store with my spreadsheets.

"See you tomorrow, Mr. McDonough!"

Out in the parking lot, the air was finally getting nice and warm and I took a deep breath. When I exhaled, I heard someone calling "Niiiiiiiiiiiiiiick!" It was Pink calling. Pink from the neighborhood, from high school, Pink who'd worked one year at Walmart before coming in stoned and getting fired and losing all his benefits. He still shopped there, no hard feelings. He was wearing an enormous gold watch and pushing a stroller with a sleeping baby that had jelly on its face.

"Niiiiiiiiiiiiiiick!" he yelled. "Nick!"

He shook my hand hard, with deep feeling, like we were

long-lost friends who hadn't seen each other in years. I'd seen him two weeks ago.

"Did you hear what happened to Chip?" he said, holding on to my hand and looking at me with half-sad, half-sober eyes.

"What happened to him?" I asked.

But I suddenly knew what had happened to him. I could hear my voice crack as I spoke—"What happened, Pink?"—and I felt queasy, wobbly, happy to be grasping Pink's soft hand as I saw my friend Chip lying six feet six facedown in a ditch somewhere on the other side of the world. And here he had just emailed me, saying it was boring and there was nothing to worry about, and I'd believed him. I'd said there wasn't going to be a war, and he'd believed me. And now Joey Joey was on his way there, to that same war, all smiles and lipstick and papers signed.

"He got called up for the army," Pink said. "You didn't hear?"

I withdrew my hand. "That's old news, Pink," I said. Pink always had old news.

"I need a job, Nick," he said amiably, pushing the stroller into the store.

"That's old news too," I said.

That weekend I went to the going-away party that Joey Joey's mom was throwing. The grill was on when I got there and so was the music. There were nieces and nephews crawling around in the backyard, and his mom had strung red-white-and-blue streamers all through the house and tree.

"Well, look who's here," his mom said. She was fatter than last time, and she was wearing a T-shirt that said, HOLD STEADY. She hugged me hard. Her arms went around my neck. She was doughy and it felt good. "Get yourself a plate, Nicky," she said. "Get yourself a beer."

Joey Joey was on the deck with everyone I hadn't seen in a long time. Everyone had put on weight. The flag was out and it was waving in the breeze. The breeze felt nice. It was going to be a nice spring.

"If more people made an effort to keep the flag out," someone said, "we wouldn't be in the mess we're in today." Everyone agreed.

"You look good, Nick," someone said. I had come from work in my white shirt and was overdressed for the occasion.

"Nick's a businessman now," Joey Joey said. He winked.

"Can you get me a job down there, Nick?"

"What about me, Nick?"

"Sure," I said to everyone. "Come down and fill out an application." I'd hire them. They'd work three months maybe. They'd work a year. I'd fire them.

I ate a hot dog and I drank a beer. The beer made me tired. So did the sunshine.

"You look tired, Nicky," Joey Joey's mom said. I felt like sitting down but there was nowhere to sit except the ground.

"Nick's always tired," Joey Joey announced. He was reclining luxuriously in a blue chaise longue with the back put down to the last notch. He'd bought it at Walmart. Everything in the backyard he'd bought at Walmart, including the grill and including the flag. The rest he'd bought when he sold drugs.

"Nick runs the store," Joey Joey continued. The way he was lying in the chaise, the center of attention, all comfort and ease, with one arm behind his head and his shoes off, speaking *about* me but not *to* me, made it seem like he was big man around town again.

I ate another hot dog.

"You got ketchup on your shirt, mister," one of the little cousins said. In the middle of my white shirt, right near my heart, was a red stain about the size of a thumbprint. "You look like you got shot, mister," she said.

Everyone thought this was funny.

"Bang bang!" she said. "Bang bang!" The words were infectious, and all the little cousins and nieces and nephews, everyone under the age of ten, ran around the yard, screaming, "Bang bang! Bang bang!"

I was ready to leave. I waited fifteen more minutes and then I kissed Joey Joey's mom goodbye. "It was good seeing you, Nicky," she said. "Don't be a stranger." Then confidentially, she said, "Thank you for everything you've done for Joey Joey."

"Aw," I said, "I haven't done anything much for him." Which was kind of true.

Joey Joey said he'd walk me out. We passed through the kitchen, where his sister was making a bowl of pasta salad. "Are you leaving already?" she said. She was five years older, her hair had highlights, and her nails were so long she had to grip the serving spoon with her palm. She'd visited Joey Joey every day when he was in jail.

"Nick's a businessman," Joey Joey said again. "He's got spreadsheets to work on." He thought this was funny.

But out on the porch he got quiet, he got melancholy. We stood around with our hands in our pockets, looking at the traffic go by.

I said, "You're about to go on an adventure," and I slapped him on the back.

"Sure am," he said, but he didn't seem too excited. He was staring at the traffic.

"When you see Chip," I offered, "tell him I said hi."

"Sure will," he said.

His demeanor made me earnest. "When you get back, your job'll be here for you." It was company policy, but it sounded like I was doing him a favor.

"I do appreciate that, Nick," he said.

"You're welcome," I said.

Then he turned and I saw those eyes again, wide, white, tense. I could have been staring at him through a jailhouse window.

"I don't want to die, Nick," he said.

The sentiment caught me off guard. "You're not going to *die*." I was oddly offended.

"I don't want to die," he said, as if he hadn't already said it.

"You're not going to die," I said, louder now, like I demanded it. I was angry and also embarrassed. "You have a greater chance of dying in a plane crash," I said, because that was what the statistics had shown.

He was nodding and taking deep breaths as if he was trying to catch up to the absurdity of his panic. He smiled a brave smile. Then he hugged me unexpectedly, putting his arms around my neck and pulling me close. He was doughy like his mom, but he was stronger than I expected, and I felt at his mercy. He held me long enough for it to begin to feel awkward. When he released me, we stood staring at each other.

Then, to lighten the mood, I grabbed him by the shoulders. "Kick some ass, Private!"

On Sunday, when I pulled up in front of the shop, Zlottie didn't look as if she thought she was going on a date. She was dressed in that same black blouse with that same black skirt and those same black shoes. She looked like a witch. Or a mortician. It was going to be seventy degrees and sunny, the first day that year we were going to hit seventy degrees, and I couldn't imagine she'd be able to stand the heat for long, especially considering we were spending the day at the amusement park. "I've never been to the amusement park," she'd told me, clapping her hands in delight. I couldn't believe it—twenty-six years old and never been to the amusement park.

Still, she had dressed like this.

I got out of the car and opened the door for her like a gentleman. Her father was nowhere to be seen, so I thought I'd start the day off right by giving her a kiss on the cheek, but she giggled and moved past me and sat down and slammed the door closed herself.

I took the bridge. I drove slowly. I wasn't in a hurry. I'd been up early again, trying on different outfits: dressy, sporty, casual. In the end, I decided on jeans and a tank top. I wanted her to see my arms and shoulders, just like I wanted to see her legs and ass.

"Down there," I said, indicating the river, "is where I used to go fishing." I'd only gone fishing once, the time we caught Zero the turtle.

"Fishing!" Zlottie said. "I've never been fishing."

It sounded like an invitation for an invitation. "I'll take you sometime," I said. I glanced at her to see if the promise of a future engagement had made an impact. She was staring down at the river. "I've never been fishing," she repeated. "I've never been to the amusement park. I've never been to a ball game."

All her life in this city and she'd never been anywhere except BILDMAN'S SH P.

The entrance to Adventure Playland was clogged with strollers and soldiers. The park had become all the rage again because they'd built a new roller coaster called Kingdom Coming and everyone wanted to see if it lived up to the hype. Up and down in sixty seconds, the commercial said. The commercial ran every fifteen minutes. It had been ten years since I'd been on a roller coaster, any roller coaster, and I couldn't wait.

At the ticket booth, I bought two all-you-can-ride passes for thirty dollars.

"All you can ride?" Zlottie said with apprehension.

I bought a hot dog for myself but nothing for her because: "I can't eat anything here, Nick, you know that."

"Aren't you going to be hungry?"

"No."

"Aren't you going to be hot?"

"No."

The line to Kingdom Coming was long and it wrapped

around the fence twice. You could hear the coaster before you saw it, a big whoosh of air, and then a few moments later a long train of red cars coming past the fence in a blur, one hundred miles per hour, jammed with people screaming their heads off.

"Wow!" I turned to her in excitement.

"I'm not going!" Zlottie said. Her face was filled with terror.

I took her hand in a comforting fashion. She let me hold it for a moment and then she took it away. "We'll come back a little later," I said.

At the far end of the park was a minor wooden roller coaster from the old days; it had a couple of hills and a few turns and there wasn't much to it. It was the first roller coaster I'd ever gone on, but I'd outgrown it and moved on to bigger and better thrills. Apparently everyone else had outgrown it as well, because no one was in line.

"I'm scared," Zlottie said.

We took our seat in the car. The car was wooden, and it looked like it couldn't go faster than a bumper car. "Don't be scared," I whispered, and I imagined putting my arm around her shoulder and holding her close. Onto my palm I briefly mapped the course that the ride would take. "See?" This seemed to settle her, but as soon as the attendant came by to push the rubber restraining bar in front of our waist, Zlottie repeated, "I'm scared!"

It was too late now, the train was starting up, clanking and groaning as it climbed that first little hill. "See?" I kept saying. "See?"

We crested tranquilly, and for a moment I could see the

whole wide city. Over there was Winchester Parks, and in the other direction was where I lived, and in the middle was Walmart with its big blue roof, where I'd be back tomorrow morning at seven-thirty. And then we dropped.

I hadn't remembered the drop to be so sharp. It seemed as if the wheels had lifted from the tracks and we were pointing straight down, hurtling toward the ground below. The momentum pulled me from my seat and I was sure I was about to be thrown from the car. I grasped the restraining bar. "Hold on, Zlottie!" I screamed in anguish. The car hit the bottom of the hill headfirst, a jarring landing that snapped me back into my seat and banged me against the wooden backrest, giving me only a second to catch my bearings before we went tearing around the bend. Now it felt as if I would be hurled out sideways against the railing that was inches from my face. "Whatever you do," I screamed, "hold on!" Around another bend we went, nearly perpendicular to the ground, with the terrible roar of the wind in my ears, the terrible screeching of the fragile dilapidated fifty-year-old wheels on the track. And just beneath the roaring and the screeching, just beneath the screaming and the pleading, I was surprised to hear the familiar sound of Zlottie's laughter. It was long and loud and without pause. Up the hills and down the hills she laughed, *wheeeeeeeeee,* through the tunnel and around the curve, and when we pulled into the finish line and the restraining bar released us mercifully into the world, she said, "Let's do it again!"

Her face was flushed and healthy. Her black hair was blown across her forehead and mouth. If her hair was fake, it didn't act fake.

I stumbled from the car. I wobbled. I belched. I was reminded of the hot dog I'd eaten.

No, I could not do it again.

"Come on," she said, "Kingdom Coming!"

"Let's sit on the bench for a minute," I implored.

We sat in the shade and I leaned forward on my elbows, fearing I might puke.

"I thought you liked roller coasters," she said.

After a while I felt her hand rest on my bare shoulder. It was a very light touch, almost incidental, but it had a reviving quality. "Come on," she said, "we'll come back later."

We meandered through the park as I tried to gather my bearings. The park was getting crowded. Every once in a while, I would hear someone calling "Niiiiiiiiiiiiiiiick!" And I wondered what they thought of me walking around with a Jewish girl.

"You know everyone," Zlottie said.

I knew everyone and she knew no one. All her life in this city and no one called her name.

As we passed by the arcade, an old guy in the booth said, "Why don't you try to win something for your girlfriend?"

I appreciated the word "girlfriend," so I gave him five dollars for three chances to make one basket. I missed all three because the ball was rubbery and the basket was steel. I gave him five more dollars, and this time I won a small stuffed purple bird with plastic eyes.

I gave it to Zlottie.

"That's ugly," she said.

"That's not the point," I said.

"Give it to a little girl," Zlottie told the guy in the booth.

He took it from her. "She's a tough lady to please," he said.

I walked on, disheartened. When we turned the corner, there was Kingdom Coming again, looming above us with its six loops and its mile-long course.

"Are you ready, Nick?" she said. "All you can ride!"

"Sure," I said, "I'm ready," but I wasn't ready. "How about we go in here first?" And I pulled her into the entrance of one of those old-time rowboat rides that goes down a dark tunnel populated by plastic gnomes who gaze out at you from nooks and crannies. It had scared me as a boy, then it had bored me, and now it revealed itself to be what it was intended for: a place of romantic possibility.

This was the destination everything had been leading toward. This was the place and the moment.

"It looks dumb," Zlottie said.

"It's not dumb," I said, "it's sexy."

Zlottie got in and grabbed the oars, but they were nailed to the sides. "I can't paddle?" she said.

"That's not the point," I said.

Through the tunnel we floated. It wasn't very dark, and it smelled like mildew and urine. The gnomes looked at me in their overalls and cowboy hats.

"I feel *so* sexy," Zlottie said sarcastically. She laughed. In the tunnel, it sounded like fifteen Zlotties laughing.

I sighed. I brooded. I said finally, "I'd like to be more than just friends, Zlottie."

"More than just friends?" She repeated. She peered at me curiously in the dim light.

"Can we be more than just friends?" I asked.

"Sure," she said, "I have lots of people who are *more* than just friends." She started naming names, a long list of names, men and women, all Jewish-sounding. I got the sense that she didn't understand what I meant by the word "friend." She probably didn't understand what I meant by the word "more." Or "just" or "want."

"Do you know what I mean?" I interrupted. "Do you know what I'm asking you?"

She squinted her black eyes at me.

It was so daunting. Everything was daunting, everything was a task. Even defining the word "friend" was a task. Even that took effort. Never mind a kiss. Never mind the first time I tried to put my hand up her long black blanket of a skirt. It was exhausting to think about. It made me want to fall asleep in the rowboat. In ten years, I'd lost my zest for roller coasters. In ten more years, who knew what other changes I'd undergo, what other passions I'd lose. I'd be thirty-six years old, still trying to fit into jeans and tank tops. But I'd be the district manager.

We floated on. The gnomes grinned at me. If the paddles had worked, I would have used them to smash the gnomes one by one. I shifted in my seat with aggravation, and as I did, the rowboat rocked hard, side to side, as if it might upend and toss me into the putrid water. I put my hand out to steady myself, but instead I accidentally caught Zlottie's wrist, and suddenly I was pulling her close to me, not thinking just doing, putting my naked arms around her shoulders, and kissing her on her lips. And damn if she didn't respond by putting her tongue right in my mouth as if she'd been waiting all along to do just that. She put her tongue in my mouth and one hand on my leg, so high up my leg that if she went one more inch higher, it wouldn't be my leg anymore. She might never have been outside Bildman's shop, but she knew what to do.

We held each other close, body against body, no countertop between us, and I ran my fingers through her hair. It was fake hair all right, no doubt about it, stiff and synthetic in my fingers like the bristles of a brush, and it smelled faintly chemical.

"I've always loved your hair," I whispered. And we floated in our little rowboat out into the sunshine.

The line to Kingdom Coming wrapped three times around the fence. We held hands and stood close and waited. Every ten minutes we'd hear the sound of the wheels rumbling, and then the train would come flying past our faces like it was shooting up to the moon. Each time Zlottie would gasp with glee and I would tremble with horror.

We moved a few steps. We waited. We held hands. We moved a few more steps.

Eventually she had to pee, though she hadn't drunk a thing. I watched her ass swish away in that black skirt.

The second she was out of sight, I heard someone calling my name. "Niiiiiiiiiiiiiiiiick!"

Who could it be but Pink again, pushing that same stroller with that same baby, still sound asleep and its face smeared with jelly. He was wearing another enormous watch, this one with diamonds, and he shook my hand hard, with deep feeling, as if he hadn't just seen me. He looked at me with half-sad, half-high eyes. "Did you hear what happened to Joey Joey?" he said.

"That's old news, Pink," I said.

"He's dead," he said. "He got killed."

He said something else I think, a couple other things, but I couldn't hear too well because the roller coaster was coming over my head with everyone screaming, and it drowned out the sound. All I could make out were Pink's lips moving inside his face, thin lips and bad teeth, jelly in the corners of his mouth. When the roller coaster was past us, he held out his hand again and we shook. He did all the shaking.

"See you around sometime, Nick," he said, and he wheeled his little baby away.

I stood there for a while. Not thinking anything, just standing there. And then I took out my BlackBerry and I checked my email. I don't like checking my email on my day off. My inbox was empty anyway.

"The line moved up, mister," someone said behind me, and I saw that the line had moved up.

I turned off my BlackBerry and put it in my pocket, but once it was in my pocket, I took it right back out and turned it on and started typing. "I regret to inform," I wrote in the subject line.

I wrote about how I had just received the tragic news that Joey Joey had been killed in the line of duty. I wrote in business-speak because that's the way you have to do this when you're an assistant manager. I wrote some nice things about Joey Joey, about how he was a good worker, about how he was going to be missed. I ended it by saying, "Condolences to all the associates."

When I was done, I didn't read it over, I just sent it out. I sent it to every one of my contacts. Five hundred people I sent it to, including the district manager. Sure enough, half a minute later it came right back to me. "Fwd: I regret to inform."

"It's our turn, Nick!" Zlottie was saying. She was standing next to me, looping her arm through my arm, and guiding me up the stairs to where Kingdom Coming sat waiting.

We took our seat in a shiny new soft black car. All the kids were chattering in anticipation, and all the grown-ups were chattering too. An attendant came by to secure us with the thickest restraining bar I'd ever seen and which clicked into place with a mechanical precision.

"Are you ready, Nick?" Zlottie said.

"Sure am," I said, and a few seconds later I could feel the contraption engage and the vibrations begin, and then the entire train, with all fifty-some people aboard, slowly started to crawl up that very first slope, as if we were merely setting off on a placid and uneventful journey.

A BRIEF ENCOUNTER
WITH THE ENEMY

To get to the hill you have to first take the path. The path is narrow and steep and lined with trees that are so dark they could be purple, and so dense it feels as though you're walking alongside a brick wall. You can't see in and you hope that no one can see out.

The first time I went up the path, it was terrifying. I could barely take a full breath, let alone put one foot in front of the other. If I'd had to run, I wouldn't have remembered how. Besides, I was loaded down with fifty pounds of equipment that clanged and banged with every step. I might as well have been carrying a refrigerator on my back. But after the first month, the fear dissipated and the path started to become fascinating, even charming. I was able to appreciate the "beauty of the surroundings"—as the brochure had said—even the trees that I was constantly bumping against. "What kind of trees are these?" I asked out loud. I wanted to learn everything I could. I wanted to get everything there was to get out of this experience.

"Christmas trees," someone answered back. He was being funny, of course, and everyone laughed, even though we were missing Christmas.

The sergeant wanted to know what was funny. We told him nothing was funny, sir. He said that that was true—nothing was funny, that if you could get shot in the face at any moment, then nothing could be funny.

So we were quiet again, the fifty of us, we were fearful again, but that didn't last too long, because fear can't persist unless you have at least a little evidence to sustain it. Fascination can't persist either. What can persist, however, is boredom. I had come all this way hoping for something groundbreaking to happen, and nothing had happened. Now twelve months had passed, and tomorrow I was flying back home.

That's what I was thinking about when I walked up the path for the last time.

I was also thinking about Becky. "Ooh," she had said when I told her the news. "You're going on an adventure, Luke!" She'd clapped her hands like a little girl. "I sure am," I said.

We'd run into each other in the lobby. She was coming down with a cigarette and I was going up with a sandwich. I hadn't seen her since the afternoon I'd tried to casually ask her out and she'd said no, point-blank. "Do you want to get some ice cream?" I had said. I'd known her since high school, and the Mister Softee truck was parked right outside.

"No, thanks," she'd told me. "I'm on a diet." I couldn't tell if that was an excuse. Her body looked fine to me.

Six months later, though, she was all smiles, standing close to me in the lobby and batting her eyelashes as the other office workers came and went around us in a big wave of suits.

I was deploying in two weeks, but I tried to make it sound as if it was no big deal. In fact, it *was* no big deal. Everyone thought that the war was coming to an end. Everyone thought that it was only a matter of time. We'd taken the peninsula and we'd secured the border and we'd advanced to within twenty-five miles of the capital. Any day now, everyone said. My main concern had been that I wouldn't make it over in time to see any action.

She said, "You going to keep in touch, Luke?" And she made a pouting face, as if I'd been the one to turn down her invitation for ice cream.

"You know I will," I said.

She had big lips and long lashes. She had a little gray in her hair, but I didn't care about that. She'd been married and was now divorced. I didn't care about that either. I'd just hit twenty-seven and was getting soft around the middle. I was hoping to get back in shape. "Push yourself to your physical limits," the brochure had said.

She wrote her email address in purple ink on the bottom of my sandwich bag. When she walked off, I took a long look at her ass. She didn't need a diet.

In the first couple of months, I made a point of emailing her. We were each allotted fifteen minutes a day at the Internet café, and I sent her updates when I could.

"What's going on down there, Luke?" she wanted to know. "Tell me everything." She ended her emails with "xoxo* * *."

"What's that mean?" I had to ask one of the guys.

"Hugs and kisses," he said.

"But what do the asterisks mean?"

He didn't know.

There wasn't much to report about what was going on. The enemy had yet to make his appearance. So I told her that we had an Internet café, and a bowling alley, and a Burger King. "They have everything down here," I wrote.

It wasn't entirely true. They didn't have things like boots. It was the rainy season and it rained every day. To be fair, there were ponchos, but ponchos don't keep you from slipping and sliding when you're going along the path on patrol in Skechers. If you got caught in a particularly bad downpour, you might as well be ice-skating, and you'd come back to base at least an hour late. The sergeant would mark this down in his blue book. He'd make sure you saw him marking it down. What happened after that was anyone's guess. "You get ten of those, you get court-martialed," the most paranoid among us speculated.

Boots did finally arrive. This was about three months into our tour. They came from Timberland, no less, donated free of charge so that not everything would have to fall on the taxpayers. Half the guys sold their boots right off; they sold them to the other half of the guys who could afford to buy them and have two pairs. Then they used the proceeds to purchase things like cigarettes and instant soup. There was a guy named Chaz who wanted to give me twenty-five dollars for my boots.

He acted like he was doing me a favor. "I'll tell you what I'll do," he said. He sat down on my cot and took out his money. "Whaddya say?" He was trying to be chummy about it. He was trying to be down-home. He'd gone to a good college and his parents sent him money every two weeks and we had nothing in common except that we both wanted boots. He was one of those guys who had joined for all the wrong reasons. He had joined not because he believed in anything but because he wanted to put it down on his résumé and jump-start his career.

I told him, "You're here for the wrong reasons, Chaz."

He said, "What reasons are those?" As if he didn't know.

He used phrases like "in the long term" regarding my boots. Twenty years from now, I'd probably see him on television, asking for my vote.

I emailed Becky to tell her that we'd gotten new boots from Timberland.

She emailed back:

But what else is going on? xoxo***

It wasn't the rainy season now. It was the hot and dry season. No one needed boots anymore. I made it to the end of the path in fifteen minutes. I could have done it in flip-flops. I could have done it barefoot.

It was getting close to evening, and things were cooling down a bit, but the flies were buzzing and I was sweating badly because I was dressed as if I were heading into battle. I felt less like a soldier and more like I was going trick-or-treating dressed as a soldier; all I needed was a bag for my candy. Everything about me was superfluous and ridiculous—the boots but also the helmet, the jacket, and the backpack, which rattled on my back like a gumball machine. The gun was unnecessary too, but it was the lightest thing on me. That was the contradiction. It was three feet long and looked like it was made of iron, but it felt like plastic. It could have been a squirt gun, except for the fact that it had all sorts of gadgets and meters on it that told you things like the time and the temperature. Plus it could kill a man from a mile away. You hardly even had to pull the trigger. If you put your finger in the proximity of the trigger, it sensed what you wanted to do and it pulled itself. *Poof* went the bullet, and the gun would vibrate gently, as if you were getting a call on your cell phone.

The first time I'd ever shot a gun was when my dad had taken me and my sister down to the woods to go hunting. This was about ten years ago, when the war had just started. There were supposed to be things like deer and elk lurking around in those woods. At least that was how it had been when my dad was a kid and his dad had taken him hunting. But times had changed, and the factories were up and running for the war effort, and the woods had been dug through to make way for a new train line. Not only were there no deer or elk, there weren't even any chipmunks. So instead of teaching us how to hunt, my dad drew a bull's-eye on the side of a tree using a piece of chalk. Inside the bull's-eye he drew the face of the enemy. It was a surprisingly good representation, although he exaggerated the nose and eyes and ears for comic effect.

"This is how you hold it, Luke," he told me. "This is how you cock it. This is how you aim it."

I remember that the gun was heavy like a brick, and when I pulled the trigger, it felt as if my right hand and ear had caught on fire. "Look what you did, Luke!" my father screamed. Sure enough, I had hit the bull's-eye right in the center. "Try again, Luke," he said, but I didn't want anything more to do with it.

My sister, on the other hand, had a great time. She blasted away at the target, *blam, blam, blam,* pretending it was really the enemy. Most of the time she missed everything, including the tree, but she thought the experience was fun and funny. "He's dead!" she kept saying. "The enemy's dead!" She looked like a pro, even though she was only twelve. I threw stones in the river, waiting for the shooting to be over so I could go back home and play video games. By the time evening came and the bullets ran out, she'd blasted a hole through the tree.

"They're all dead," she said.

Ten years later, it was the sergeant asking us if we wanted to end up dead. No sir, we said. He had us at target practice two hours a day. Lying on our bellies, crawling through the mud. We were training like mad because we thought we were going to be doing some real fighting. One week after we arrived, the war had taken a turn for the worse, just like that, and there was no longer a chance that it was going to be ending anytime soon. We had lost the peninsula and we had mishandled the border and we had been forced back from the capital. Each day the reports would come through listing the number of casualties. It always seemed to fall somewhere between two and two hundred, and by the time word spread around the base, no one could be sure if the numbers were being exaggerated up or down. It was anyone's guess how many we were losing. I say "we," but we had nothing to do with it. We had landed on the other side of the country, far from the fighting, and we hadn't lost anything—it was the poor bastards a thousand miles away, trying to push back toward the capital, who had something to worry about.

I wrote to Becky a few times: "Can you tell me what is happening, please?" When her email came back, it would be almost entirely redacted:

██████████████████████████████████

████████████████████████

xoxo***

According to my state-of-the-art gun, it was now 6:02 and eighty-five degrees. Back home, it was twelve hours earlier and sixty degrees colder. Tomorrow morning we were flying home, and we didn't care that we were going back to cold weather. We were flying home on American Airlines, which had donated the plane free of charge. "Traveling in style," the guys said. They said that it was the least American Airlines could do. The fact was that twelve months had passed and we hadn't done much of anything. Our main accomplishment might have been the bridge that I was walking across. My boots echoed in the valley. It was sturdy, the bridge, and it was steel, and it would no doubt be here, sitting at the end of the path, in ten thousand years, when the war was finally over. We had built the bridge in order to get across the valley. We had to get across the valley so we could get up the hill. The hill was the goal. The hill was where the enemy was waiting for us.

"Eight hundred and eighty hiding," our sergeant had told us. How he'd come up with that number, we didn't know. It was so specific, we thought it must be true.

Ten hours a day we worked on that bridge. We'd wake up in the morning when it was dark, and we'd eat our powdered eggs in darkness, and by the time we walked up the path and reached the valley, the sun would just be rising, and the light would seem to be emanating upward from the valley, golden and warm, with traces of pinks and reds. One of the guys, who worked at a used-car dealership, said that if he was going to make a car commercial, he'd use the valley as a backdrop to portray things like power and eternity, and everyone said that was right, that they'd buy that car for sure.

But the truth was that no one really wanted to get the bridge built, because no one wanted to get over the hill. We didn't say this out loud; instead, we worked as slowly as possible, and as incompetently. We accidentally dropped tools into the valley. I once dropped my blowtorch. It slipped from my hands like a bar of soap and bounced down the cliff until it took flight into the abyss.

"Do you know how much that blowtorch cost?" my sergeant screamed. He screamed like the money was coming out of his own pocket. He screamed like I had dropped his daughter in the valley. He stared at me for so long, one inch from my face, breathing like he'd run a race, his breath smelling like powdered eggs, that I thought he was actually asking if I knew how much it cost.

"A hundred and thirty-five dollars?" I guessed.

This caught him by surprise. "It cost forty dollars," he said.

That didn't seem like all that much.

"I should drop *you* in the valley," he said. He made me do push-ups, right then and there, thirty push-ups. I got down on the ground, but I couldn't do them. He told me to take my backpack off and try again, but I still couldn't do them. This pissed him off even more. He put me to work cleaning the bathrooms, which was fine by me. I could have scrubbed toilets for the rest of my tour and been perfectly content. I could have scrubbed toilets for the rest of my life. Anything not to get over that hill and find eight hundred and eighty enemy waiting. But the next day I was back working on the bridge, bright and early. He needed all the help he could get. His superiors were probably screaming at him an inch from his face. Their superiors were screaming at them, and so on and so forth, until you got all the way up to the president screaming and panting as if he'd just run a race. Meanwhile, on the other side of the country, the casualties were mounting.

Day after day, we hammered and welded. Fifty guys pounding at the same time. The sounds echoed through the valley from morning to night, so that if the enemy didn't know we were coming, they knew now.

One night, one of the guys said that we should go on strike. He was a farm boy from Iowa or Idaho, big and pink. Half the guys were farm boys. The other half were black boys. There was a smattering of others, like me and the future politician, but those were the basic demographics.

"Put down the tools of your trade, men," the farm boy said. He'd heard that somewhere.

"I'm not putting a damn thing down," one of the black boys said. "I'm trying to learn a skill." Then he whispered to everyone, "I pay attention. I ask questions. I watch every-thing." He made it sound as if he were planning to rob a bank. Which, I suppose, is how you feel when you've joined the army not because you have beliefs but because you want a job.

So we spent the better part of four months working on that bridge, but even when you work slowly and incompetently, you make progress. And when we arrived at the other side of the valley, we couldn't help but have a twisted feeling of pride. Yet the moment we stepped off the bridge and faced the hill, we knew we had entered no-man's-land. We had colluded in our own demise.

The hill wasn't like the path. It was rocky and gray with no growth and no place to hide. It looked like a giant bowl of uncooked oatmeal. It looked like a place you could easily bury fifty bodies and no one would know.

"No time like the present," the sergeant said. And we put our backpacks on and our visors down and we raised our guns and started up.

The truth was that none of us had joined for the right reasons. I might have thought I had in the very beginning, when I'd gone to the Career Center to sign the papers and take the physical and get the brochure that promised a "life-altering experience" and showed half a dozen young men in uniform standing on a beach and looking like they were having the time of their lives. It was easy to delude myself because every-one was congratulating me for living up to my ideals. Who would want to argue with that? There were three hundred people at my going-away party at work, chanting, "Luke!

Luke! Luke! U.S.A.! U.S.A.!" There were people there who had never said a word to me, who had never so much as looked at me in the hallway, including the managing director. Now they were acting like they'd known my name all along, like I was a movie star making a guest appearance at their company. All the guys were shaking my hand, and all the girls were kissing my cheek. The managing director gave an impromptu speech about "men like Luke," and about how my job would be there when I got back in a year, because that was company policy. It was the most boring job in the world, and I didn't want it to still be there when I got back. I was sure that something miraculous was going to happen to change my situation and make me into someone new. All I did was sit in a cubicle eight hours a day, five days a week, staring at a computer as I filled in the little empty blocks on a spreadsheet. *Click, drag, drop. Click, drag, drop.* Half the time there wasn't anything to do, and I would sit there staring at the blank screen, pretending that I was working and wishing I could go online and look at porn. *Click, drag, drop.* This is what happens when you have an associate's degree.

But at my going-away party, I soaked up the applause. I thanked the managing director for all his support. I thanked everyone for coming. They stood around smiling and waiting for me to say something special, something profound. Three hundred people staring at me with my face covered in strawberry lipstick. Then someone in the back yelled, "Shoot some of those motherfuckers for me, Luke!" That broke the ice and made everyone laugh, and we sliced up the big red-white-and-blue cake they had all chipped in for.

It wasn't until the moment when we started up that hill

that I understood I'd come here for all the wrong reasons. Vanity and pride topped the list. Girls too—if I was being completely honest. In other words, ideals were very low. Staring at a hilltop that was getting closer and closer, I would have traded all of it never to have to see what was on the other side.

When we got to the top, the sergeant at our rear, we peered over like scared little boys, our heads low and our eyes half closed, and that was when we realized there was no one there. Not a soul. All that existed was a wide-open space, a prairie almost, bordered on one side by a lake and on the other by more prairie. It surprised everyone, this desolation, including the sergeant, who wanted to move up front and commanded us to follow him into the great unknown where there was no sign of life.

That first day we explored and came up empty. The next day twenty-five guys went back to discover nothing. After that, fifteen guys went, then ten, then it was decided the exploration was a waste of time and energy, that the reconnaissance had been wrong and the enemy was nowhere around, and all we needed was one guy to go along the path and over the bridge and up the hill once a day to make sure there was nothing out of the ordinary.

Which was what I was doing that last day as I neared the top of the hill. It was 6:43. It was still eighty-five degrees.

After we'd discovered nothing was when the boredom set in. Excruciating boredom. We'd eat, we'd shower, we'd clean, we'd train. In that order. Then we stopped training, because there was no point. That was about the fifth month.

During the sixth month, I went to the movie theater almost every day. Something had gotten mixed up in the supplies, though, and the theater had only two movies, both *Indiana Jones*, one of which was dubbed in Spanish. I watched them over and over, even the Spanish one, and then I never went back. A couple of the guys asked the sergeant if we'd be getting any more movies, and his response was "You're worried about movies when our boys are being killed a thousand miles away?" He had a point.

The days dragged on. Instead of getting in shape, I started to get fatter. If I ever let myself reflect on matters of spirit or psyche, I reflected that at the end of my tour, all I would have to show for my effort was that I was one year older. In short, I was going to get out of the army and be exactly the same person I was before I joined. I was going to go back to that same cubicle with those same spreadsheets. At night I dreamed of fantastic adventures, full of action, shot in vivid color, not unlike the *Indiana Jones* movies. I dreamed of being possessed by exceptional courage and heroism. I dreamed of confronting the enemy. In the morning I'd wake with disappointment, eat, shower, clean the dorm, and then go bowling. My bowling improved.

Becky would send emails saying that she was worried about me, wanting to know what was going on, wanting to know if I was okay. Eighty percent of her messages would be redacted. For a while I fanned her concern by responding with ambiguous statements like "We'll just have to wait and see." Soon her concern started to make me feel foolish, and I stopped going to the Internet café as often. When I did go, I would use my fifteen minutes to look at porn.

About the only thing we could do for the war effort was cheer for the planes that flew overhead on their way to drop their payload on the other side of the country. They sounded like thunder when they appeared, always around noon, two dozen or so, their bellies silver and red. We'd jump up and down, fifty of us guys, screaming at them, waving our arms as if we were on a desert island, hoping the pilots would give a signal that they'd seen us. In the evening they'd pass back going the other way, flying faster because they were lighter.

One day our sergeant said, "What are you waving at them for? There's no one in those planes. Those are drones."

I came to the top of the hill. It was 7:12, according to my gun. It was starting to get dusky and gray. I stood and surveyed the great expanse of nothingness. North to south, as I had been trained. Then east to west. The water, the prairie. Nothing.

It was silent up there on the hill, except for the occasional buzzing of the flies. It was always silent, but today even more so. I had a surge of nostalgia: this was the last time I would be standing here. It was similar to the phenomenon that prisoners experience, becoming nostalgic for their cells the moment they are released.

I unzipped my backpack and took out my meal, which came in a little plastic container with an American flag. It was dinnertime, but I hadn't eaten my lunch yet. Today it was ham and cheese with an apple and a cookie. Yesterday it had been turkey and cheese with an apple and a cookie. Tomorrow I would be making my own lunch. Two days after that, I'd be back at the office in a cubicle looking at spreadsheets. I sat down on a rock and ate my sandwich. The flies buzzed. I felt nostalgic for the army lunches.

And it was then that I saw him. At first I had no idea what I was seeing. At first I thought it might be an animal. All I could detect was some faint movement way out in the prairie, maybe a mile away, a rustling of the grass. It's just the breeze, I thought. But as I continued to watch, I saw the unmistakable shape of a human head appear above the tall grass. I put down my sandwich and picked up my backpack. My hands were shaking as I took out my binoculars, and I had to clamp my elbows together to steady my gaze. Sure enough, there he was. A tall, bald, fat man, maybe fifty, maybe younger: the enemy.

He was walking with something, a sheep or a goat, I guessed, although I could scarcely see it in the grass. I imagined that he was moving stealthily, the man, that he was trying to keep himself concealed, but when the grass parted, it was clear that he wasn't trying to hide from anyone. It was as if he had gone out for an afternoon stroll. His nonchalance irritated me. It flew in the face of my boredom. Everything I had done for the past twelve months had been in relation to this man's existence—or nonexistence—and now here he was, seemingly unperturbed by what lay beyond the hill on which I was sitting. He didn't even know we had built a bridge.

He was moving toward the water, perhaps bringing the goat or sheep to drink. I watched the man carefully through my binoculars. It felt slightly invasive to be watching him so closely, slightly pathetic. Years ago, I had made the discovery that a window in the hallway of my apartment building faced the bedroom window in a neighboring apartment. I was probably about ten years old and had just grown tall enough to be able to peer over the high window ledge. The bedroom belonged to a woman, and I remember that she was rather disappointingly plain, and that she had long plain brown hair, dishwater hair, and she dressed always in baggy pajamas, sacklike, that revealed nothing. All she did was lie in bed and read. For hours she read. For hours I would stand there in the hallway watching her, hoping she would do something exciting, like take off her clothes and masturbate. But she read, and I watched. And then around ten o'clock she would put her book down on her nightstand and turn her light off and I would go back to our apartment, where my father would ask me what I'd been doing for the last two or three hours in the hallway.

"Nothing, Dad," I'd say. Which was true—I'd done nothing.

Standing there now on the crest of the hill, I did something: I picked up my gun and released the safety. I hadn't handled the gun in a while and it felt strangely heavy, unwieldy even, as if I were trying to hoist a manhole cover with my bare hands. It pressed down painfully on my shoulder as I peered through the sights. The man was standing at the edge of the lake, and he was peeing. He had his hand on his hip and he was leaning backward in a posture of bliss, and his face was not all that different from the face my father drew on that tree years ago.

I observed the man in the crosshairs. He was 1.1 miles away. He was five feet ten inches tall. He jiggled himself dry, buttoned up, and started to walk leisurely along the edge of the lake back toward the prairie. Soon he was 1.2 miles away.

Then he turned in toward the plains, toward the high grass, and just when he was about to disappear for good, I put my finger in the proximity of the trigger. *Poof.* The gun vibrated gently with its message.

He stumbled and fell face-first onto the ground. It happened so quickly that I thought he must have tripped over something. Surely it couldn't have been because of me. But no, a small pool of blood began to form under him as he lay there.

The sheep or goat that had been by his side was not a sheep or a goat after all but a little boy. He darted around in a panicked circle. I watched him through the crosshairs. His mania increased until it looked as if he might actually begin to dig a hole in the ground with his feet. He disappeared into the high grass, only to return a moment later to lift the man's arm and try to drag him off. He couldn't, of course, and for a moment I had the thought that I would run down the hill and help the boy. I would help the boy and then I would send an email to Becky telling her what I had done. "Dear Becky, Today I helped one of the local boys."

Poof.

The boy fell right where he stood, he fell straight down as if he were melting into the ground in a puddle of blood. Once he'd fallen, he didn't stir. Only the man was moving now, struggling to push himself up, but it was obvious that he had no strength. Eventually he stopped altogether and just lay on the ground as if he were napping. The pool of blood spread out and ran into the high grass.

I stood there for a while. It was beginning to get dark. It was 7:53. Back home, it was the other 7:53. A few minutes later, the prairie was immersed in a dark gray light and I could hardly see anything. The only sound was the buzzing of the flies.

I turned and went back down the hill, the last time I'd be going down the hill, and then I went across the bridge and along the path. My gun and backpack banged against the solid wall of trees. It was almost completely dark, and in the dark I could hear my father saying, over and over, "What have you been doing, Luke? What have you been doing for the last two or three hours?"

Nothing. I've done nothing.

The next day we flew back home in style, just like we'd been promised.

ENCHANTMENT

It was cool weather when I returned. Cool, breezy, overcast, but no rain. I had departed in cool weather too. So in some ways it was as if nothing had changed.

What had changed was that I was a hero, coming home to great fanfare—me and one thousand other guys. We were lucky to have been included in the first wave back. This was when the news was fresh, when everyone was excited. Just like that, the war had ended. No one had seen it coming and everyone was thankful. The diplomacy had been a success, the enemy had capitulated, and all the terms of the settlement were in our favor. Everyone said it had been worth it. Everyone said they'd do it all over again.

Underneath a gray and cloudy sky, the boulevard was lined with ten thousand people who had come out to greet us, ten thousand people screaming their heads off like we were a rock band being pulled by in a flatbed truck. "We love you," they shouted generally. "We love you too," we shouted back. We smelled like sweat and mildew and fatigue. Some of us smelled like vomit. It had been a long trip home: a boat, a train, a plane. On the final flight we'd had to hold our duffel bags on our laps with the air vents blowing warm air on the tops of our heads, but no one complained, no one said a word, we were all happy to have made it out alive.

My mother had said she'd come out to cheer for me. She'd bought a big sign custom-made at Walmart. WELCOME HOME JAKE, it read. She showed it to me later, unfurling it on top of her bed because her place was small and there was nowhere else to put it. She was surprised I hadn't been able to pick it out of the crowd. I was touched, but she was disappointed. "I was so sure you'd see it!" I tried to let her down easy. "It was a sea of people, Ma," I said. A sea of flags and signs and waving hands. The fact was, I hadn't even thought to look for her. I'd forgotten about her, actually. Instead, I'd been searching the crowd for Molly. It had been eighteen months since I'd seen her. Eighteen months of emails filled with declarations of love, declarations of what might have been and what might be. We knew our relationship would probably never amount to anything, but still we dreamed. Fifteen thousand miles away from each other, we waxed poetic and romantic, and sometimes we sent naked pictures. The last email I'd received had been three days earlier, four-thirty in the morning Molly's time, letting me know that she was coming to the homecoming, honey, that she wouldn't miss it for the world, that she was bringing Lola. Lola wouldn't miss it for the world. And by the way, she'd attached a drawing she'd made that night, that very night, three people in watercolor, presumably the three of us, all pinks and purples and shadows. The girls wore skirts and I wore camouflage. What did I think? she wanted to know. It wasn't what I had dressed like, but it was well done. "It's beautiful," I wrote back.

"Do you really mean that?" she responded. She had confidence issues.

As the flatbed truck moved slowly down the boulevard, I jostled with the other guys for that prime position front and center. Every so often I would think I'd hear her in the crowd, yelling, "Jake, Jake," and I'd wave my arms in the direction of her voice, and I'd jump up and down as if I'd won a big prize. But there was no one yelling "Jake, Jake," they were yelling "Hey, hey" to all of us. Still, I stood front and center. "Come on, Jake," the guys said. "Give someone else a chance." But I was selfish and wouldn't budge. I'd earned the right. I'd trained harder, marched longer, fought better. The guys would have said so themselves. Plus I'd saved a few of their lives along the way. But the peace was upon us now. "It's every man for himself," I told them. It was a wonder how quickly the sense of camaraderie could evaporate.

Far out over the heads of the ten thousand fans, I could see the factories sending up their plumes of smoke into the overcast sky. You couldn't distinguish the gray smoke from the gray sky. For as long as I'd been gone, the factories hadn't stopped once. Twenty-four hours a day, seven days a week, the smokestacks churned. "I'm going to get a job down there," one of the guys said. Brad. He wasn't speaking to me, he was speaking at large. "Good luck," I told him. He needed luck. It was a fact that half the guys were going down to the factories first thing in the morning to put in an application. Everyone had a plan, and that was their plan. As for me, I didn't have a plan. I didn't need one. I was coming home to a good job, secure and with full benefits, teaching sixth-grade history at the best school in the city. Montgomery Prep. On Monday morning I would show up bright and early in my tie and briefcase, as if nothing had changed, as if I'd never left, and I would say, "Good morning, boys and girls . . ." And they'd want to know all about where I'd been and what I'd done and what I'd seen. But there would be schoolwork to undertake. And schoolwork came first. They'd be studying the Renaissance by now. Or if the substitute teacher had been inept and inefficient, which I suspected she had been, they would have made it only as far as the Middle Ages. Or worse, the Holy Roman Empire. It didn't matter to me. I was happy to get back to any era.

Eighteen months earlier, I'd had to abandon another class of sixth-graders unexpectedly, unhappily, midterm—Han Dynasty—with only three days' notice. They'd gathered around and hugged me goodbye. They'd said, "We're going to miss you, Mr. Mattingly!" I tried to be reassuring, but all I could think about was what terror lay in store for me. Everyone thought I was a hero, teachers included, but the reality was I had no choice in the matter, it was the deal I had struck in exchange for my college degree when I'd had the forethought, two weeks out of high school, to go down to the Career Center and sign up. I didn't want to end up like my mother, working as a telephone operator for thirty years. The recruiter had told me they'd need me one weekend a month unless there was a war. "But there ain't going to be no war," he'd said. He had laughed. We both had laughed. I'd signed on the dotted line and then gone straight down to Peabody Community College to register for fall classes—all paid in full by that one weekend a month. It had seemed comical back then, the idea of a war. It had seemed antiquated. Three years later it wasn't antiquated anymore, and three years after that my number had come up. Now this trip down the boulevard, with the flags waving, with the crowd screaming, represented my final remittance.

And suddenly right then and there, standing in the front row behind the police barricade, not more than a dozen feet from me, waving one of those small ninety-nine-cent American flags that you could buy at any supermarket, was Molly. I saw her before she saw me. Her red hair was loose and long, longer than it had been before I'd left, and it was cascading down her shoulders like a lion's mane. She was wearing a sweater because it was breezy and cool, but there was an extra button unbuttoned that allowed me to see the tops of her breasts. She had small breasts and a big butt, which I liked. "It's all going to waste," she'd written me, two months into my deployment. The truth was, we'd hardly ever had sex. Maybe ten times total. Twice in my car and the rest on my futon. She'd regretted all of them. "I'm sorry, I'm sorry," she'd sobbed the last time. She'd put her face in her hands and her hair fell forward. I wasn't sure if she was sorry about the sex or sorry about being sorry. I'd tried to put my arm around her shoulder to comfort her, but she shrugged me off. She told me she preferred me as her muse, not her lover. I had no idea what that meant. "From now on," she said as if making a declaration, but didn't bother to finish the thought. She tried it for a while—muse not lover—but physical affection cannot be forestalled forever, and eventually she started holding my hand again, and then kissing me, and three weeks before I deployed, she put her hand down my pants. Thirty minutes later she was sobbing. Now here she was, as promised, standing in the crowd, looking intense, concerned, almost despairing. She must have been waiting at least two hours for my return, studying the faces of the floating one thousand. She no doubt had reached the point when she was certain I had passed her by. "Here I am, Molly!" I wanted to shout, but I didn't say a word.

Just to her right was Lola, grinning, waving to anyone and everyone, unmoved by her mother's dilemma. It was all fun and games to her, this parade. Her umbrella was open, even though it wasn't raining, and she was resting it on her shoulder, twirling it like a little woman. I was stunned at how much taller she'd gotten since I'd seen her last. If it hadn't been for her own red hair, I wouldn't have recognized her. She'd been a girl when I left, six years old, interested in girly things, dolls and teddy bears; now she was close to nine and tending toward women's things. "Here I am, Lola!" I thought about shouting. But no, I didn't say a word, because standing beside her, which is to say between her and her mother, was her father, tall and thin and gullible. His face was friendly and welcoming and wealthy. He was clean-shaven. He was clueless. He wore a baseball cap that said U.S.A. He had one hand around Molly's waist, squeezing her proprietarily, and with the other hand he waved generously at the passing soldiers. "Thank you! Thank you!" he called. There had been only a handful of times when I'd seen him in the flesh, and every time had left me both despairing and emboldened. His presence brought him out of the realm of conjecture and into the solid world, where he eventually would be vanquished.

When it came my turn to receive his thanks, I did so, lifting my hand and waving in return. "Thank you! Thank you!" he shouted naïvely. It was then that Molly saw me. Her face registered shock. Her shock turned to relief. The relief turned to love. I smiled at her as I would at any bystander. Then the truck moved past for the last leg home.

The manual said that I'd most likely experience some aftereffects from the war once I got home. But the first thing I had to do was reclaim my efficiency from Fred the subletter. He was clearly disappointed to see me return. There were no accolades forthcoming.

"I wasn't expecting you" was what he said. He was probably hoping I'd been killed.

He'd taken decent care of the place while I'd been gone, as well he should have. I'd given him a sweet deal. Somehow he'd managed to leave a palm print on the ceiling in the kitchenette, but other than that I could find no wrong. The apartment was smaller than I remembered, and more cramped. I had thought it would feel bigger after eighteen months away. After all, I'd been living on a military base with five hundred other soldiers, sixty-two to a room, twenty-two to a shower. In the middle of the night I'd be awakened by the sound of everyone snoring.

"How was it, Jake?" Fred wanted to know, meaning the war.

I was sure he didn't care, and I didn't care to tell him. I offered a cliché: "Fred," I said, "I'd do it all over again."

He liked that. "Thank you for your service," he said.

He gave me the last month's rent in cash. I wanted to count it in front of him, because I didn't trust him, but I waited until he left. The sun was starting to set, and it cast shadows in thin gray lines across the apartment. I call it an apartment, but it's a room, a square room, fifteen by fifteen with a kitchenette off to the side. I sat down at the table that doubles as a desk, and I counted the money. It was all there, in tens and twenties. It made me feel rich. The feeling of wealth helped to mitigate the feeling of claustrophobia. I spread the bills out on the table. It was the same table where I graded my papers and ate my meals and read my newspaper. If I folded the leaf up, it could be a table that sat six for dinner. I couldn't even fit six people in the apartment. On the wall was a drawing that Molly had made for me, framed and signed, of a man sitting at a table looking at a drawing of a man sitting at a table. "I like to work in meta," she'd said. It had been done in charcoal and like everything else she did, it was very good. Sitting there staring, I realized that I'd developed a half-shaped, half-conscious idea that when I returned from the war, I'd be returning to a house. Maybe Molly's house. When you're fifteen thousand miles away, it's easy for things to seem possible and attainable. I could have been at her house in twenty minutes. I'd once driven by on a whim, dinnertime, just once, pretending to myself that I had some errand to run in her neighborhood. Her proximity was terrifying and tantalizing. I could have walked right up and rang the doorbell. Instead, I'd parked across the street and sat in the car. I didn't even turn the radio on. Her house was grand. It should have been grand, her husband was rich. It had a wraparound porch, it had a balcony off the master bedroom, it had a swing set in the yard. For thirty minutes I sat in the car waiting for something to happen, something like Lola coming out and swinging. Every so often I would catch a glimpse of a figure passing in front of the bay window, but the shade was drawn halfway and I was never certain who it was. Later Molly told me, "Don't ever do that again."

But I don't really mind my apartment, it's the nicest apartment I've ever had, and I've had many. We went from apartment to apartment, my mother and I, a succession of apartments, small, big, lousy—roaches, no roaches—on average a new apartment every two years, and one year it was two in one year. That was when times were hard. That was when I was a child. Now I'm an adult with a dishwasher and central air.

It turned out that Fred wasn't the only one unhappy to see me return.

"Where's Mrs. Tannehill?" the sixth-graders wanted to know.

Mrs. Tannehill was the substitute the school had hired to take my place while I was gone. She was elderly, fifteen years past retirement, still bouncing from school to school, trying to piece together a living. She had arthritis and perfect diction.

"I do so love children," she'd told me before I left, as if she weren't doing it to make money.

"Who doesn't love children?" I'd asked her. I was being snide, but the question had made her beam.

She obviously knew something about teaching, though, because the children weren't behind in their lessons. That Monday morning I'd been surprised to walk into the classroom before school began and find the walls covered with drawings of the major figures of the Enlightenment. Spinoza. Locke. Newton. They were already on the Enlightenment.

On the floor beneath the drawings were cardboard dioramas in shoe boxes, a dozen or so dioramas featuring pivotal scenes from three centuries ago, like the apple hitting Newton on the head. I'd never done dioramas with my class. I'd never even considered them.

She'd also been conscientious enough to leave a detailed report on my desk, written in exquisite, outdated penmanship, informing me of each student's strengths and weaknesses. "Ellery is shy, analytical, easily flustered. Mallory is contemplative, creative, and has allergies . . ." I didn't bother to read the whole thing. My main concern was the prospect of having to rework my lesson plan, which had been handed to me six years earlier like a baton by the retiring history teacher, and which went only as far as 1959. "You won't ever make it past 1910," he'd sniggered. He'd been right till now. At the rate the students were going, they'd make it all the way to the present.

The day had started with such promise. I'd had butterflies coming around the bend, seeing the school in the early-morning light, two stories in red brick with a chimney. It was idyllic and beautiful, the school, in a run-down, affluent sort of way: drafty in the winter, hot in the summer, mice in the basement. It was surrounded by woods, a pond, and a baseball field, which had, when I'd driven up, six sprinklers going full force, trying to keep the grass green and lush. The school had been built one hundred years ago, when everything was corn and wheat. Since then it had produced three congressmen and one poet. Their portraits hung in the lunchroom as a reminder. "Give your best, get your best" was the school motto, etched above the main entrance. And that morning the principal, Dr. Dave, had been standing beneath the portico, waiting to greet me personally.

"Here comes the soldier-teacher!" he cried. He shook my hand vigorously. He looked me in the eye.

"I'm glad to be back, Dr. Dave," I said. I wanted to sound easygoing, but I was ecstatic that he was taking time out of his day. He wasn't much older than I, but he was more successful, and that always plagued me. It put my life's accomplishments into perspective. He'd gotten his doctorate by twenty-six, he'd become principal by twenty-nine, he spoke Japanese. He wore jeans every day to prove that he was down-to-earth. He went by his first name, but with "Doctor" added for the constant evocation of academic achievement. The day I got the news of my call-up, he'd appeared unannounced in the teachers' lounge and said a few impromptu words about "Jake's decision to become a soldier," ending with "Give your best, get your best." I'd always found the phrase fatuous, but it had made me blush like a boy.

It was only seven-thirty and the students hadn't arrived yet and everything was quiet. Dr. Dave escorted me down the hallway with his hand lightly on my arm. My arm felt muscular beneath his hand. Our footsteps echoed on the stone tile. Here comes the hero.

George the custodian was mopping the floor. He'd been

mopping the floor for twenty-five years. When we passed, he stopped and said, "Welcome back, Mr. Mattingly."

"I'm glad to be back, George," I said.

"I prayed for you every day," he said. He was being obsequious, and I liked it.

The typing teacher came out of her classroom and said, "Oh my God, Jake," and hugged me. It was the first time a woman had touched me in eighteen months and I thought about resting my head on her shoulder. Her voice filled the hallway, which brought the spelling teacher out of her room, and the art teacher, and the English teacher. They all came running. Soon the hallway was filled with two dozen teachers and George, standing around waiting for me to regale them with war stories. I gave them platitudes. I told them it had been an honor and a privilege. I told them I'd do it again. They enjoyed the platitudes. They mistook the platitudes for details. Dr. Dave raised my arm like a boxer who'd won the championship.

But an hour minutes later I had fourteen boys and girls staring at me, wanting to know where Mrs. Tannehill was.

"Mrs. Tannehill was your substitute," I informed them.

Their faces were blank. They didn't understand. A substitute was someone who *replaced* the teacher. They had begun the year with Mrs. Tannehill, who was now being replaced. The seventh-graders before them had only ever known Mrs. Tannehill as well. As far as everyone in the near vicinity was concerned, *I* was the substitute.

The students sat in two rows of five and one row of four. They were the children of those who could afford prep school tuition—bankers, lawyers, doctors. They would grow up to be bankers, lawyers, doctors. This was the cycle and I was a part of it. They dressed in clean, pressed uniforms in the school colors of gold and black. The girls wore dresses, the boys wore ties. Their ties were gold or black. They might have appeared like well-behaved students, with their hands crossed, their pencils at the top of their desks, but their expressions were vindictive and mistrustful. They wanted me gone.

I explained to them that Mrs. Tannehill had been covering for me while I'd been "off fighting a war." This was supposed to impress them, but it made no significant impact, even on the boys. It left me at a total loss as to what to say or do next. I'd been prepared for a rousing reception from these twelve-year-olds and now there was silence. Perhaps they thought I was inventing my military service. No doubt they'd grown accustomed to being lied to by adults. It would have helped if I'd been wounded in the line of duty, just a minor wound, something that had left a mark. I could have rolled up my sleeve and said, "This is where the bullet went in." There was a soldier in my battalion who lost the tip of his pinkie finger. Brandon. It was only the tip and only the pinkie, and he'd done it while cleaning his gun one morning. He was an idiot, but it wasn't a gruesome disfigurement, nor would it hinder him in life, and it was something he would forever be able to tell an unprompted story about. In lieu of my own wound, I thought about passing around my military ID, but that struck me as defeatist and emasculating. No, they wanted something tangible. They wanted the tip of my finger.

I tried a different angle. "Who here can tell me how the war ended?" Even as I said it, I could hear the honeycoated quality of my voice, pedantic and condescending. It was too late to take it back. I was talking down to them and they knew it, asking them a question that even a five-year-old could answer. Still, I waited, arms crossed in the pedagogical style, looking for someone to provide me the correct response, which, of course, was "We won." This was the pivotal moment that I had studied in my teacher training courses; it was where I would gauge if the students respected my authority and viewed me as an educator. All I needed was one child, one out of fourteen, to give me the answer and I'd be able to move on organically to a discussion of what I'd been doing the last eighteen months. They would demand descriptions and I would give them descriptions. All the brutal descriptions their hearts desired. I'd hold nothing back and they'd be spellbound. Death by drowning, by burning, by whatever means available. That was how we had won the war.

While I waited, I could feel a prodigious amount of silent time slipping past. My mind wandered dangerously. It began to fade. I realized how jet-lagged I was. The manual had cautioned about fatigue. I became absorbed in the dioramas, little resting Newton being crowned by a clay apple, and I contemplated what historical events came after 1959 and how much work it would be for me to piece those events together. Through the window, I could see the gray sky hovering over the edge of the woods. The sprinklers oscillated across the baseball field, *shuck, shuck, shuck* was their sound, their reach long and powerful, and most of the time they missed the field altogether and shot straight into the pond.

Finally, mercifully, a little girl in the back row raised her hand. Her name was Bethany and she wore a gold ribbon in her hair and sat with perfect posture. "Bethany is bright, introspective . . ."

"Yes, Bethany?" I said.

"Is Mrs. Tannehill sick?"

It was three weeks after I'd gotten home that I was finally able to see Molly. It was supposed to have been only two weeks, but that's the nature of an affair. We'd had a few phone conversations along the way, breathy and furtive and yearning, and each time she'd had to hang up in the middle. "I'm trying my best, honey," she'd promised. But she didn't seem all that bothered. This was not how I'd envisioned my homecoming.

She arrived on a Saturday afternoon with Lola. They were en route to a pottery class and had one hour to spare. Lola leaped into my arms straightaway. At least she was happy to see me. "What'd you bring me?" she wanted to know. She was heavy in my arms. She'd become a little woman. I wanted to bury my face in her neck and weep at the passage of time. I wanted her mother to see how much I had missed them.

"I was at war," I said. "I didn't bring you anything."

She shrugged. She jumped from my arms onto the futon. She jumped up and down on the futon. The futon was pushed against the wall and doubled as a couch, in the same way that my desk doubled as a table. My kitchen cabinets doubled as a place to file papers. This was life in an efficiency. With three people it was crowded.

"Don't jump on the bed," Molly said.

"It doesn't matter," I said. I wanted to be permissive.

Molly let me kiss her on the cheek. It was a casual, platonic, meaningless kiss that I had perfected. Molly wanted to make sure Lola was protected from the effects of "our transgression." If Lola were ever to innocently mention something to her father, it could be explained away as a harmless kiss from a harmless friend. "Mommy's old friend Jake." "Mommy's dear friend Jake." That was the parameter we worked within. We'd been working within it for three years. In three years, Lola had never said anything to her father. She seemed to notice nothing and be affected by nothing. As far as I could tell, she seemed to love me. I often wondered if she loved me most of all and was aiding and abetting us, perhaps unconsciously, because I was the one she really wanted as her father. "He's absentee," Molly had told me when we first met. She didn't mean that her husband traveled, she meant that he was emotionless and humorless. He was an entrepreneur. He owned shopping malls or shopping centers. "I'm trying to help the world," she said he'd tell her. He spent his weekends on the phone.

We sat around my desk/table, the three of us, eating muffins that I'd bought for our reunion. Lola wanted to eat only the tops of the muffins. "The muffinheads," she called them. She pulled them apart, stuffed the heads in her mouth, and put the unwanted portion back on the plate. She was disgusting.

"Eat the whole thing," Molly instructed.

"It doesn't matter," I said. I wanted to be the good guy.

Six muffins later, Lola had to use the bathroom. The moment the door was closed, I pulled Molly onto my lap. Her body was warm and her hair fell in my face. "No, no, no," she cooed, but she straddled me anyway. She was always sure to offer resistance. The resistance only increased the desire, of course, but it seemed to put her mind at ease and resolve the moral dilemma.

She'd married too young. That was the dilemma. She'd had Lola too young. That was another dilemma. She'd wanted to be an artist—now she was thirty-eight and a housewife.

"It's too late," she'd tell me.

"No," I'd say, "it's never too late." But I didn't really believe it myself.

We'd met by chance at a museum three years ago. She'd had her sketch pad and I'd had my students. I'd brought them on a field trip to show them a traveling exhibit of antiquities from the Ottoman Empire. They were disinterested and I was distracted. Molly kept walking past with her high heels and her hoop earrings and her red hair. I tried my best not to have my students catch me looking at her ass. I'd shown off in front of her by doing an imitation of Mehmed II. The class had roared and she had smiled. They loved me, those students. They would do anything I wanted, answer any question I asked. As we were leaving, I happened to run into her at the coat check. "If you ever want a guided tour . . ." I said. I had no idea she'd take me up on it. I had no idea she was married. A week later we were back at the museum. She'd brought her sketch pad again. In truth, she was the expert, telling me about the artwork and the artists and the brushstroke. She showed me some of her own drawings. They weren't of paintings and sculptures but of people looking at paintings and sculptures.

She was obviously talented. "They're amazing," I said. "Do you really think so?" she said. We sat close to each other in front of Monet's water lilies while she talked for twenty minutes about the painter's failing eyesight. I was fixated on her hip pressing against my hip. Later we made out in my car, and when we were done, she pulled her wedding ring out of her pocket. It had one huge diamond. "I've never done anything like this before," she said. She thought that would be the end of us, but it wasn't. I didn't care about any nameless, faceless husband. It was every man for himself in this world.

We'd seen each other about once a month since then, sometimes twice a month. We avoided phone calls, we deleted emails, we met at out-of-the-way places. Once, when her husband was preoccupied, we managed to see each other two days in a row. We took Lola to the circus on Saturday and the amusement park on Sunday. It was like we were a family, or trying to be a family, laughing and sliding down the water slide. It had seemed like a grand achievement at the time not to exhibit any trace of desire. "Mommy's friend Jake."

Now Molly was on my lap. Her legs wrapped around me. Her skirt rode up high.

"Come back," I gasped.

"I will," she whispered.

"When?" I asked.

"Soon," she said.

"How soon?"

By the time Lola came tearing out of the bathroom, flinging herself on my couch/bed, and screaming, "Let's play war!" Molly and I were sitting in our respective seats talking about the weather. We were pros.

* * *

The days were getting longer and warmer, but the sky was overcast and it still hadn't rained. To get to school each morning, I drove over the bridge heading east. Down along the river, I could see the factories all in a row, their smokestacks going. A few of them had closed since the war had ended. That was an unintended consequence of the peace. The people who had come in from the outskirts for work were heading back to the outskirts.

As for my classroom, it was established that the students hated me. Even those Mrs. Tannehill had described as "loving," "caring," "forgiving" loathed me. In the beginning I tried to curry favor by handing out candy from a large glass jar that I kept on my desk—a blatant disregard of teaching ethics—but it didn't achieve the desired result. The children would eat the candy sullenly and in a manner of obligation. I had become the enemy in their eyes, and even when the enemy gives something good, it is received with suspicion and resentment. Naturally, I began to hate them in return. I fantasized about failing them, each and every one. I would fail them through no shortcoming in their classwork, but it would serve them right all the same. I would teach them a lesson about the vagaries and the violence of the real world. Unfortunately, failing them would require more work from me than passing them. It would require written explanations and conferences with parents. Dr. Dave would want to know what had gone wrong and where. In the end, it would be simpler to pass them. A's across the board. But those A's would come at a price. There would be no drawings, no dioramas, no excursions to museums. No candy. In short, no fun. That would be our pact. If I were the enemy in their eyes, then I would play the role of the enemy.

Meanwhile, they made quick work of the American Revolution, the French Revolution, the Victorian Era, the Great Famine. Decades fell by the wayside. Their collective rigor and acumen were impressive. They wrote thoughtful, insightful essays about the reasons one million people had to starve to death. Their grammar was excellent, their spelling perfect. I could find no fault. The twentieth century loomed. It wasn't until the Civil War that I managed to bog them down. War made their shoulders slump and their eyes glaze over. I punished them all the more for it. I spent whole classes standing at the front of the room, reading aloud from eyewitness accounts about Harpers Ferry and Bull Run—"Yonder down below, I descried a figure . . ."—trying to draw subtle, meaningful parallels to our present. Other times I copied long passages verbatim from the textbook onto the chalkboard, and as I copied, they copied. For an hour the only sounds in the classroom were the scraping of chalk and pencil and the sprinklers going *shuck, shuck, shuck*. On Thursdays they read aloud, on Fridays they read to themselves. On Mondays I turned obscure. "Who was General Zollicoffer, Chloe?" Chloe didn't know. Chloe must memorize. "Where was the Battle of Pea Ridge, Trevor?" Trevor must study more.

"History is dead," I said one day, apropos of nothing. "The past doesn't exist." I slammed the textbook closed for emphasis. The idea had come into my head fully formed. I thought it sounded profound, but the students looked weary. I opened the jar of candy on my desk and took out a handful. They had not had any in quite a while. I jiggled it in my hand as if considering. They stared at the bounty. I went from desk to desk, slowly giving one colorful piece to each student.

The enemy sometimes gives spontaneously and for no apparent reason.

They unwrapped their treats reflexively. They stuck them in their mouths. They waited for the bell to ring. They thought of Mrs. Tannehill.

It was during the Gilded Age that Dr. Dave showed up one morning unannounced. I was content with the Gilded Age. I had slowed the class perfectly, and with summer vacation approaching, we would have enough time to dip a toe into the twentieth century. That was all we needed to do in order to say we had done it. Then they could go on to seventh grade.

"Is it okay if I sit in today, Mr. Mattingly?" Dr. Dave asked. There was a hint of agenda in his voice.

"Of course it is," I said. But I was ill prepared for observation. I made a grand sweep of my arm toward a desk in the back, as if my hospitality were immense.

I instructed the class to welcome Dr. Dave and they obliged mechanically: "HEL. LO. DOC. TORRRRRR. DAY. VE." I scanned my students' faces, trying to determine who among them had betrayed me. Someone no doubt had said something to their parents, who had called Dr. Dave. He had decided to come investigate for himself. The first thing he was sure to notice was the jar of candy on my desk. It glowed multicolored and bright.

He took a seat in the back row with his blue jeans. He was too large for the desk and he crossed his legs, trying to find purchase. He waited. The students waited. They knew something was amiss. They sensed my predicament. The enemy was being watched. Crimes would be revealed. As the bromide goes, the enemy of your enemy is your friend. Dr. Dave may very well have been the students' enemy too. He had it in him. I had observed him once bring to tears an eighth-grade girl who'd made the mistake of referring to him as "Mister."

"Good morning, Mr. Dave."

"I worked very hard for my doctorate, young lady," he'd explained, inches from her face.

So we stepped lightly, the students and I, we groped for détente.

I loosened my tie and smiled. They smiled in return. I asked if they had plans for the weekend. They murmured some response.

With small talk depleted, I broached the subject of the Gilded Age. "Who here can tell me about the Gilded Age?"

There was a great, wide silence. I had overwhelmed them with too broad a question. They couldn't have responded if they had wanted to. My technique had ignored the principles of how a young mind was equipped to think. Begin with relatable details, work toward larger concepts, expand outward into interpretation. It took everything I had not to glance in the direction of Dr. Dave. It took everything I had not to open the jar of candy.

"Who here can tell me," I tried again, "about the life of Cornelius Vanderbilt?" Again silence. I had whittled the era down to the size of one human figure, though I wasn't sure whether the students would have given me an answer even if they had one.

The enemy was hunted. The enemy was cornered. The enemy would capitulate. Now was not the time to show mercy.

It was warm in the classroom and I was beginning to sweat. To buy time, I took off my jacket and hung it on the back of my chair. I was sure that patches of sweat were visible around my armpits. One of the drawbacks about teaching in a quaint one-hundred-year-old building was that no provision had been made for air-conditioning. When the temperature rose, we suffered for it. The best you could hope for was that George the janitor would bring you a fan. Outside, the sprinklers toiled over the baseball field, but the grass was turning brown. Grass all over the city was turning brown. Rain was what was needed.

On the last day of the school year, Dr. Dave summoned me into his office. "Can I have a word with you, Jake?" is how he asked. I'd been expecting something of this sort but hadn't prepared an able defense.

His feet were on the desk when I walked in and his diplomas were on the wall. He was dressed in a black suit with cuff links in the shape of mortarboards. Today was graduation and presently he would be standing onstage handing eighth graders their diplomas, intoning to each, "Give your best, get your best."

It was strange to see him in a suit, and he looked severe. Severe like a magistrate. I took a seat across from him and waited for what no doubt would be an unfavorable verdict. He was dressed to inflict maximum punishment.

"I have a proposition for you, Jake," he said without pre-amble. Then he launched into a strange and roundabout story—interrupted periodically by the ringing of his phone—that had nothing to do with my lack of pedagogy.

He was looking for a house-sitter.

Now that the war was over—"Thanks to you, Jake"—he would be doing some traveling. He was going to see the world. He and his wife. They were leaving in a few days. Day after tomorrow, actually. He had lined up a house-sitter—a friend of a cousin—but that person had fallen through at the last minute because he was young and irresponsible. Dr. Dave had thought of me. I had popped into his head. Would I be inter-ested? There was no money, of course. "But I'm sure you could use your own sort of vacation, Jake." We laughed together at this. He knew my salary. He probably knew the size of my apartment. All that was required of me was to collect the mail and water the garden. Other than that, I would have the run of the house, including the forty-two-inch high-definition television.

"Do you want to think about it?" he asked. No, I didn't want to think about it.

I called Fred the subletter the next day. This time he was happy to hear from me. He showed up with a dozen boxes and the first month's rent in cash. My mother was there, helping me pack. It was her day off from answering phones and she had nothing better to do. There wasn't much to pack except clothes.

"We'll be out of your hair in no time," she told Fred. She was always apologizing for things that didn't require apology.

"If you forget anything," Fred said to me, "you're always welcome to come back."

"I know that, Fred," I said.

By the time we left, he was reclining on my couch/bed with his shoes off and his arms behind his head as if he had been the tenant all along.

Dr. Dave's house was located an hour away, on the other side of the river, in the exclusive and upscale Cranberry Township. In the car, I gave my mother half the rent money.

"Oh, I don't need that," she said. She took it anyway.

Fifteen minutes into the drive all traces of the urban world were gone, replaced by the countryside. The countryside would have been picturesque, except it was wilting. I'd been to Cranberry Township once, when I was a boy, eight years old maybe, visiting a friend I'd made at day camp. Rodney. It had been a summer day but we'd spent our time in the basement playing video games and eating potato chips. In the evening his father had driven me home in his Mercedes-Benz. I'd had the idea that I would be returning to Cranberry Township shortly, but twenty years had passed.

"All I'm saying," my mother was saying, "is it's wrong." She was complaining about the war. The second wave of soldiers was coming home and apparently no one cared, including me. This is why it's good to be first.

"It's just not right," she said, "it's not good." It was a sign of bad things to come. She paused, waiting for me to agree with her. I turned the radio up louder. After a while she started humming along, one hand tapping out the rhythm on her thigh. Her thighs were getting thicker. Her hair was getting grayer. She'd be retiring soon. She'd end up with back problems and a decent pension. Suddenly she turned to me and said, "How's your girlfriend?" The word "girlfriend" reverberated within the confines of the car. I couldn't tell if she was using the word ironically. I couldn't tell if she knew something. That was always one of the concerns with having an affair: you never knew who knew something.

She'd seen Molly once by accident. We'd gone to the movies together, Molly and I, on one of our clandestine romantic outings, and my mother happened to be sitting in the back row. I was hoping she wouldn't notice me, but she did. I introduced Molly to her as my girlfriend. It had slipped out inadvertently. I'd never used the term before or since. "It's a pleasure to make your acquaintance," my mother had said with overblown formality. Molly and I sat in the front holding hands, but I couldn't follow the plot. We ended up leaving midway without my mother seeing us. She called me later to say, "Your girlfriend's got nice hair."

The farther I drove, the more the countryside wilted. The earth was drying up. The trees were losing their leaves. Brown swaths covered the hills like a disease. In Cranberry Township the houses got larger and the streets got wider and the grass got greener. The streets had bucolic names like Eagle Claw Lane and Turtle Dove Drive.

My mother said, "Looks like a fairy tale."

I turned right, I turned left, and there at the bottom of a steep hill, set back about one hundred feet behind two trees, with a mailbox and a weather vane, was my final destination for the summer: 14 Misty Morning Way.

The blue jeans did not begin to tell the story. The blue

jeans were an affectation bordering on fraud. Whatever else Dr. Dave had accomplished at such a young age, his house had to have been the ultimate accomplishment. Ivy covered two walls. The walls rose three stories. The windows were framed by wooden shutters. On the front door was the number fourteen carved in wood, and when I turned the key in the lock, the door swung open onto a foyer with two umbrellas in an umbrella stand. Stepping over the threshold, I had the sensation that everything had just changed for me, changed for the better, that I was passing through a very difficult epoch of my life and arriving at something akin to success.

My mother passed through behind me. We trod silently, cautiously. We could have been mother and son from the Gilded Age, entering their grand home. We could have been thieves.

There were four bedrooms in the house and stainless-steel appliances. There was wall-to-wall carpeting and a library. The library contained educational tomes and books in Japanese. "I'm going to do some reading this summer," I announced.

Past the library was a living room. Past the living room was another living room. Everything was pristine and flawless and spotless, including the garden, which my mother and I entered by opening a sliding glass door that had no fingerprints and made no sound.

The garden was the masterwork. It was as wide as the house and twice as long. There were trees, there were birds, there were flowers. It could have been a painting. I took off my shoes, because to walk on the grass with shoes seemed like a violation. The grass was as soft as the carpeting. It looked as if it'd been trimmed with scissors. My mother and I stood around saying nothing. The garden smelled like summer and country and rebirth, and in spite of the dry spell, Dr. Dave had managed to keep it alive. But it was more than alive, it was thriving. Add to his accomplishments horticulture.

I commandeered the house without hesitation. I'd been born for a house like this. Within days I was walking around in my underwear, leaving the toilet seat up, and eating straight out of the refrigerator. In effect, I had supplanted Dr. Dave.

Each morning I'd wake in the master bedroom to the gray light coming through the windows. I'd lounge in the king-size bed listening to the birds, thinking about how Lola would enjoy jumping on a bed like this, thinking about how Molly might want to have sex on a bed like this. Then I'd walk down two flights of stairs to the kitchen and eat breakfast in front of the forty-two-inch television. When I was done, I'd slide open the glass door and step outside in my bare feet and water the garden. I didn't use the watering can, I used the hose, generously, spraying the plants and flowers until everything was soaked through including my feet.

Around noon the mail would arrive. After the mail arrived, Molly would arrive. Lola came too. She came every time. They seemed unfazed by the new surroundings, Lola especially. The first time she entered the house, she jumped in my arms and seemed to take no notice that we were no longer in a one-room apartment. I wanted to give her a tour, but she didn't care about "any dumb tour." She was a rich little girl, after all, with a house of her own. Still, I'd expected some sense of wonder. But all she wanted to do was play. I bought her balloons and balls and a Hula-Hoop. While we played together, Molly painted. "Don't disturb Mommy." She'd brought her paints and an easel and a smock and set up her studio in the garden beneath the lemon tree. She was going to make five paintings this summer. She was going to make ten paintings. She was going to find an agent. Maybe find a gallery. Maybe have a show. Everyone had a plan and that was her plan.

In the afternoon I would grill fish or chicken on Dr. Dave's immaculate gas grill with its pushbutton ignition. I used his Japanese carving knives. I behaved like a patriarch, hoping to ruin their appetite for dinner. I wanted the memory of our day to linger long after they got home.

Afterward, the three of us would lie on our backs, sated, looking at the gray sky, while I told Lola tales from history. Archdukes and presidents and the Ottoman Empire.

"Those are boring," Lola would say.

At five o'clock they left. Occasionally Molly would put Lola in the car, then pretend she'd forgotten something, rush back in the house, and make out with me in the foyer.

"Come back."

"I will."

"When?"

"Soon."

"How soon?"

She did not come back soon. She came only a few times a week. Monday, Wednesday, Friday. That was her schedule.

That was not the schedule I had envisioned when I had envisioned my summer. Sometimes she came Monday, Wednesday. Once it was just Monday. It was never weekends.

"Where have you been?" I once screamed after five days of absence. We were in the garden, and I was unshaved, and Lola was staring at me in disbelief because she had never heard me scream before. Molly was staring at me too, smiling slightly as if she'd known it would eventually come to this. "You men are all the same," I could hear her thinking. She had one hand on her hip, cocked slightly, and one hand on her easel. She had just begun a new painting of people lying on the grass looking at people lying on the grass. I thought of grabbing the canvas and smashing it against the lemon tree.

"Would you like us to leave?" she asked. Her equanimity terrified me. I had no choice but to accept the terms.

I filled my empty days by trying to do something productive, something enriching. I selected Dr. Dave's educational tomes and took them out into the garden. The books were heavy and the reading was ponderous. Soon I would fall asleep, facedown on the grass. I dreamed once that I was heading back to war. I was on a train going over the ocean. The waves lapped at the window. "Is this seat taken?" someone was asking me, and when I turned, I saw that it was Molly. "No," I said, "it's yours," and then I watched impassively as she struggled to put her suitcase in the overhead rack. I should help her with that, I thought, but it was every man for himself in this world. So I stared out the window, hoping to spot whales in the water below. I had never seen whales before. The din of the train grew louder; it combined with the din of the ocean. Beneath it I could hear Molly saying, "It's all going to waste."

It was apparent that I did not have what it would take to earn a doctorate. It was also apparent that the solitude of the house was beginning to crush me. I considered driving back into the city, back home even, just to stop by for a minute, "just stopping by, Fred." But that seemed akin to admitting defeat. Defeat of what, I wasn't sure. I thought of calling Molly. I wouldn't care if her husband answered. "Do you know who this is?" I'd ask. "Do you have any idea?" I'd gloat. I'd preen. He'd squirm. "Who is this?" he'd demand. I'd let the line go dead.

And if she answered the phone, I'd say, "Please come."

Instead, I roamed the house with the television turned high. The third wave of soldiers was arriving home. They were having a parade to which no one was going. Only the reporters were going, and a high school band. From floor to floor I roamed. Room to room. The rooms echoed. What once felt spacious now felt vacuous. Those few things that Dr. Dave and his wife had forgotten to put away before they left to "see the world," a half-empty glass of water, for instance, began to give the impression that the occupants had been surprised by thieves one afternoon and murdered. I added to this sense of disarray. My absolute ease in their home had an insulting, apathetic underbelly: muddy footprints on the carpet, dirty dishes in the sink, hair in the bathtub. I recalled having once read an article about a gang of criminals who had invaded a vacant, wealthy house, not to steal but to live slovenly.

That's what I was, an invader, a plunderer of privacy. In one of Dr. Dave's closets I discovered two dozen pairs of identical blue jeans, hanging on hangers, ready to go. For fun I tried them on—they were too big. In another closet I found a box of photo albums. Sitting on the floor cross-legged, I looked through every one of them. Dr. Dave in the swing, Dr. Dave on his eighth birthday with cake on his face, Dr. Dave at the prom. He was born, he grew up, he graduated. And then it was his wedding day with his bride, a babe, dressed in her wedding gown and winking at the camera, her bouquet in her hand.

In another closet were his academic papers and professional correspondences, hundreds of pages, some in Japanese.

Everything that I took out, I put back exactly where it'd been. There would be no trace of my transgression. But hours later I'd be overcome with anxiety that I'd been careless somewhere, and I'd retrace my steps into the closets and trunks and boxes, fixing and readjusting.

Still, I hunted. What I was searching for, I did not know, something illicit I suppose, something secret, something that would debase Dr. Dave before the world. I found nothing. Not one thing. Not even pornography.

In lieu of nothing better to do, I masturbated one afternoon using his wife's panties. It was thrilling and empowering, but when I came, I had a clear and unobstructed view of myself, almost as if watching myself from above. There, down below, I could see a small figure named Jake standing naked in a stranger's living room in the middle of a summer afternoon with no idea what he was supposed to do next.

The flowers are dying, I thought, and I went out to water the garden.

*   *   *

Meanwhile, Molly's painting progressed. It's amazing what you can accomplish given just two days a week.

When she arrived, she would give me a kiss on the cheek and get right to work. "I don't have much time," she'd say. She meant it. She wore her smock and mixed her paints and studied the foliage. She painted people looking at the foliage. It was a theme that never tired and which she consistently improved upon. I liked thinking that the subjects in her paintings were variations of us, the three of us, but I didn't want to presume, and I didn't want to ask.

She worked slowly, cautiously, meticulously. It took hours for something even remotely recognizable to take shape, sometimes days, but when it did, it was glorious. She saw things I never noticed: snails and spiders and imperfections in the stonework. "Look at how it curves slightly. Isn't it beautiful?" Yes, now that she mentioned it, it was beautiful.

It had become my job to occupy Lola while her mother attended to the important work. Never mind that I had my own aspirations for the summer. I would wander through the rooms calling "yoo-hoo," displacing furniture as I went, further distressing the home in my game of hide-and-seek. And when I finally found Lola hidden under the bed or under a pile of dirty laundry, she'd scream as if she were about to be killed, bloodthirsty screams. I'd pick her up and swing her around. Her beautiful red hair falling in her face.

Back out in the garden, we filled balloons with water and hurled them at each other, so careful to avoid Mommy and her paintings. When the balloons burst, I would reflect on how our game was doing its part to aid the dying garden.

And the garden was dying. There was no question about it. We were presiding over its death. The plants and flowers were not able to survive the lack of rain, they were folding and drooping. Even the sturdier ones had collapsed and died, and the grass was turning brown. I blamed myself for this state of affairs, for not having been more diligent in my care. To make up for it, I fed them an inordinate amount of water, sometimes three or four times a day, sometimes in the middle of the night. "I'm sorry," I whispered. "Forgive me." My feet made indentations in the earth as I walked to and fro with the hose, spraying it like a firefighter entering a burning house. A bee buzzed around a flower, and I knew that this was how flowers were made, and I knew that I had no real understanding of the process beyond that. Bugs crawled past my feet at a glacial pace, asking not to be harmed. "I won't harm you," I said. This was the garden I would have had as a child if things had been different for me. If my mother had had ambition towards something more than being an operator. It was the luck of the draw.

And then summer was ending. Just like that. Dr. Dave was on his way home from his travels, school was about to begin, and Fred the subletter was being dislodged once more.

"Hope you had a wonderful vacation," Dr. Dave wrote by way of a postcard that arrived on a Thursday afternoon. He signed his name "Dr. Dave." There was a photograph of a winding river in some exotic locale. What river it was, I didn't

bother to look, because I didn't care. The arrival of the postcard shocked me into something resembling the present. I had
two days to pack and leave. Two days to put the house in
order, the state of which was distressing. One and a half days
really, since it was already midafternoon.

I began by cleaning the stairs, the carpet, the master bathroom. On my hands and knees, I scrubbed the tub and toilet.
Somehow I had left a dark ring around the tub, even though
I'd only taken one bath. There was a small trail of moldy spots
above the shower which I could only reach by perching pre-
cariously on the edge of the sink. When I was finished, my
neck ached, but the bathroom shone. I stayed up past midnight doing the best I could. The house was big, though, and
the more I cleaned, the more I realized how much needed to be
cleaned. If I had plundered Dr. Dave's privacy before, now I
plundered his cleaning products: Lysol and Ajax and Pledge
furniture polish. That night I slept on the couch because the
sheets and blankets were in the laundry.

It was fortunate for me that Molly and Lola arrived the
following afternoon. They found me standing in the foyer
wearing rubber gloves and holding a brush. "The lease has
expired," I said. There would be no painting that day.

To Molly's credit she helped without complaint. Lola
helped too, loading and unloading the dishwasher. She liked
pushing the buttons. The three of us cleaning made me feel
like we had come together as a family again, like there was
hope for us again.

In the pantry, I found Molly bent over sweeping crumbs
into a dustpan. I grabbed her from behind. Her ass was soft
and round.

"Come and help me make the bed," I whispered.

"There's still so much to do," she protested, but she followed. In the bedroom, the gray afternoon light was coming through the window one last time.

"So this is the master bedroom," she said. I couldn't tell if she was impressed. She had never been in it once. The realization was painful. Still, I took some pride, as if the room belonged to me.

We lay down on the bare mattress and made out. She let me unbutton her shirt. She let me feel her breasts. Her breasts were smaller than I remembered. I liked them small. We would finally have sex on something other than a futon.

"Lola," she whispered, "Lola is here."

Lola was always here, always somewhere nearby. She was the sentry that stood between her mother and me. She was the thing her mother never left home without.

"She doesn't know," I said.

"Yes," she said, "she does."

What did she know? She was innocent and oblivious. What could she know about what was happening between the adults? She could not possibly define what was going on. It was a mystery to everyone involved, including us.

But perhaps it was possible the little girl did know *something*. Something more than us even. Perhaps she only needed a few more years to be able to find the right words that would help her explain the thing—at least to herself. Twenty years from now she'd recall this as the summer she spent playing in that strange house with that strange man. She wouldn't even remember my name. I'd be a memory by then.

Molly was on top of me. Her bra was off but her pants

were on. I grappled with her belt. "No, no, no," she kept saying, even as she pressed down on my chest with her hands, bearing down as if she wanted to push me through the king-size mattress. She looked so beautiful in the gray light. "I love you," I said. I love you. I waited for her to rejoin.

And shortly there came the reply, from Lola of course, shouting up three flights at the top of her lungs, "THE DISHES ARE DONE!"

The efficiency was small again and reentry was painful. Fred the subletter shook my hand and said "Till next time, Jake," but there wasn't going to be any *next time*. He gave me the last month's rent in cash again, but I didn't bother to count it. I had more important things to do, like get ready for my first day of school. There wasn't much to prepare, of course, what with my recycled lesson plan, but I was determined to start the year off right.

The next morning I came around that familiar country bend driving fast, with the school in the early light, two stories in red brick with a chimney. I parked and got out and walked briskly. Fall was in the air. "Welcome to the history of the world!" I planned to say to my students. I had rehearsed it. It would be a dramatic opening line and it would get their attention. They'd look at me with eager, anxious eyes, not knowing what to make of me. Then I'd launch into the great migration out of Africa where it all began, thousands of miles away, thousands of years ago. We'd be allies not enemies, my students and I. In the end, they'd adore me.

As I neared the main entrance, I was surprised to see Dr.

Dave standing there beneath that eternal school motto, "Give your best . . ." Here comes the soldier-teacher! He looked tan and rested in his blue jeans. He would have stories to tell me of his adventures. "Thanks for getting the mail," he'd say. We'd laugh about it.

"Welcome back, Dr. Dave," I called. But he didn't respond. He only stared as I approached. I thought of his house, the disorder that I had wrought over the summer, the disruption, the transgression. But I had been meticulous in restoring everything to its proper place—all secrets were safe. I had made sure of it.

On the last evening, I had stood in the garden looking up at 14 Misty Morning Way, sentimental and forlorn. The only house I had ever lived in . . . Had I lived in it? Or had I merely *stayed*. Molly and Lola had already left for home, and I spent my last few moments watering the garden one final time. The poor and ravaged garden, beguiling, chaotic, struggling to stay alive. No amount of water could have offset the terrible effects of such a dry summer, but I had tried my best. These were my thoughts as I turned off the hose and squished across the soaking lawn and through the sliding glass door to get my bags of clothes. My bare feet had left little wet footprints on the carpet, but those would dry soon enough.

It was only now, walking up the stairs to where Dr. Dave stood waiting, that I realized with great and unbending certainty that it was not the heat that had killed the plants and flowers. I had drowned the garden.

OPERATORS

It was in January that Wally came back from the war. He came back to great fanfare that I felt was undeserved. He had departed to great fanfare too—which also was undeserved. I didn't tell anyone what I thought. Instead, I said what everyone said. I said it was a shame that after everything he'd been through, he had to come back to such cold weather.

It was cold that winter. It was getting colder. Each morning when my clock went off, I would lie in bed with my eyes closed and the covers pulled up around my neck, listening to sounds and thinking about life. Life in general, life in the abstract.

I could hear the salt trucks on the street below and the sound of the wind whistling through my apartment as if the place were haunted by ghosts from a thousand years ago. It was twenty degrees outside. It was fifteen degrees. It was ten.

It was going to get lower before it got higher. Everyone was saying that this was the worst winter they could remember. I had asked the landlord to weather-strip the windows but he didn't have the time, plus it wasn't in the lease, so one weekend I took matters into my own hands and did it myself, trimming the sheets of plastic, sealing them around the window frames, and blow-drying them so they tightened like a drum. But I must have been careless with my work, because the plastic sheets expanded and contracted whenever the wind blew, as if the windows were taking deep breaths. Lying in bed with my eyes closed, with the clunking and creaking all around me, I would try to puzzle out my dreams from the night before, dreams full of symbols—lightbulbs, doorknobs—dreams that seemed to ride the cusp of nightmare and lingered in the background the next day.

Each morning that January, on my way to the train station, I would buy a newspaper from the newspaper guy on the corner. "What's the word today, buddy?" I'd say.

He wasn't interested in small talk. He wore a coat over his coat. He wore a hat pulled down so you couldn't see his eyes. He wore a scarf wrapped twice around his face and tied in a knot. I paid him in change but he never bothered to count it.

The word was that the war was going to end soon. Our man had taken over. Our man had supplanted their man. Their man was on the run. We were on his tail. Any day now, the newspaper said.

Walking to the train station, I would examine the little box of numbers on the front page that outlined our progress from the day before. On our side the casualties were generally light, generally insignificant, one or two here and there, sometimes

three or four, never more than five, while on the enemy's side
the casualties were gruesome, occasionally horrific, almost always at least one hundred, sometimes several hundred, and
once, when two of their battalions had been cornered in the
valley, eight hundred and twenty-one.

Turning the corner, I would bend in half against the wind
that came off the river and caught me in the face and whipped
the newspaper in my hands and whipped under my coat and
up around my suit and tie. Up and down the street in front of
the houses, the American flags were whipping too. Far away
across the ocean, where the action was, it was warm, it was
sunny, it was seventy-eight degrees. Every day the little box of
numbers on the front page announced that it was seventy-
eight degrees, and every day we inched closer toward catching
their man, and every day I boarded the 8:02 and took a seat
next to one of the regulars, who liked to make small talk, who
said, "What's the word today, Zeke?" But I wasn't interested in
small talk. I would recline in my seat with my cup of coffee
and stare at the advertisements above my head of the handsome young men in their spotless uniforms, standing on the
beach or on the mountaintop, smiling at the camera and drap-
ing their arms around their buddies' shoulders as if they were
having the time of their lives. "You too can help," the advertisements read. "You too can make a difference." Outside my
train window, the frozen landscape of the city passed by, the
suburbs first, then the schools, the factories, the warehouses,
Walmart and Kmart, the fix-it shops, the scrapyards, the ghet-
tos, and finally, thirty-two minutes later, coming fast over the
bridge, the office buildings would appear, office buildings lit
up twenty-four hours a day, including the one that in a few

minutes I would be entering. This was the great progression of civilization.

In the reflection of the train window, I would look at my face, and I would wonder if—at the age of twenty-eight—I was still young, and if I was still handsome, and in the last quarter mile I would drift off and have a brief but vivid dream, a straightforward dream in which all symbols were apparent, in which I wasn't on a train heading toward any cubicle on the forty-eighth floor but far away, tracking down their man with my gun, with my uniform, with my night-vision goggles, getting closer and closer to the glory.

We threw a welcome-home party for him. Some of the girls spent the morning decorating the conference room with signs drawn in blue and red markers, which said things like WELCOME HOME, WE'RE PROUD OF YOU, YOU'RE OUR HERO.

When the managing director came around to my cubicle collecting money for refreshments, I gave him three dollars.

"He sure is someone special," the managing director said. I knew for a fact that he hardly knew who Wally was.

Who he was was the guy who delivered the mail, the *mailboy,* and I was the one who'd gotten him the job. It had been my job first. His father had asked me to put in a good word for him and I had. I'd known Wally since high school, where I was the valedictorian and he was a regular student in regular classes. Everyone had expected nothing from him and great things from me, but I'd made some bad choices and squandered some good opportunities and ended up having to sign on as "dispatch administrator," which meant mailboy. I'd worked three years in the subbasement, sweating in every season, before getting promoted to the forty-eighth floor. Wally had worked three months in the subbasement before he signed up for the army. Now everyone thought he was special.

"He sure is," I said to the managing director, and then I said what a shame it was that he had to come back home to the cold weather.

The managing director obviously wanted to talk more, to heap more praise on Wally, more unearned praise on someone he didn't know, but it was ten o'clock and my phone was ringing. Everyone's phone was ringing. It was time to get to work.

Bringg, bringg, the phones resounded through the cubicles, one hundred phones lighting up at once as if we were the command center for something important. *Bringg, bringg.* I watched the managing director walk away with my money and then I put on my headset and pushed some buttons the way a fighter pilot might push some buttons, and I said as pleasantly as I could, as naturally as I could, "Good morning. My name is Zeke. How may I help you today?"

Two hundred times a day I said this, exactly this, sometimes three hundred times a day. When Bruce Springsteen came to town, I said it six hundred times. It was always "good morning" until it was time for my break at eleven-forty-five, and then it was "good afternoon" until lunch at one o'clock, and after lunch it was still "good afternoon," all the way until it was time for me to pack up and go home. Throughout the office I could hear the voices saying "good morning, good morning, good morning, my name is . . ." A chorus of salutations that would last for the next eight hours and, if you weren't careful, could drive you crazy, could enter your unconscious and reappear when you were least expecting it, like last week when I was paying the cashier at the supermarket and I handed her my credit card and said, loudly enough for everyone to hear, "Good morning. My name is Zeke . . ."

I wasn't complaining, though. No one was complaining. We were lucky. We were bored out of our minds, but we were lucky. These were good times for us, flush times. Business was booming because of the war, because the factories had opened back up and everyone had jobs, everyone had disposable income, and all the concerts and circuses were coming to town.

The man on the other end of the phone wanted tickets to the circus. Tickets were fifty dollars apiece. He didn't care. He wanted six. He demanded six. He didn't say "please" or "thank you." I tried not to take it personally. He sounded like he smoked and maybe drank, he sounded like he was overweight. He was condescending about everything. He was probably one of those guys who worked in insurance, probably sat on his terrace all day, even in the cold, drinking cans of soda and avoiding his family. Now he was trying to make up for his neglect with tickets to the circus. He didn't say goodbye when he hung up.

After that it was an elderly woman who couldn't remember the name of what she wanted to buy. "Oh my goodness, what was it?" she asked me as if I'd know. She was confused by everything, she struggled with everything, she was frustrated with herself. I was patient for a while, and then I lost my patience and became sadistic, forcing her to suffer ten times over for the previous caller's coarseness. I leaned way back in my swivel chair playing dumb, not helping her with anything until she asked for it in just the right way, and then I gave her the least amount of information I could. She stumbled, she fumbled, "Um, um, um," the air went dead and I let it stay dead. I got satisfaction from her bewilderment, picturing her in her kitchen twirling with anxious fingers the cord on the rotary phone. It was fun for me. It was a diversion. This is how time is passed in a cubicle.

But when I hung up, I was overcome with guilt, choked with guilt, almost to the point of tears. I thought of my grandmother, alone in her apartment, rheumatoid arthritis, suffering for years before she died. I put my elbows on my knees, I hung my head in shame, my tie dangled down. Now it was I who needed to atone.

Next it was a girl on the line. She sounded beautiful. She sounded forgiving. She wanted to know if she could have two tickets for the Shakespeare play. "Yes, you can," I said, my voice heavy with remorse. If she had said one kind thing, anything, I would have cried in gratitude. She sounded like she was a brunette with glasses and a nice ass. I bet she was smart and read books. I bet she'd gone to a good college and utilized her opportunities. I helped her with everything she needed and I got her great seats at a good price. I wanted to ask if she was going to the show with her boyfriend. "Are you married?" I wanted to ask. I once made a terrible mistake years ago by inquiring if the girl on the other end of the line was married. This was against company policy, but she had sounded so beautiful, and my desire had been so unbearable. I'd managed to establish a rapport with her in a few minutes on the phone, and I'd kept talking to her well after sealing the deal. Just so I could talk. I didn't care about company policy, I didn't care about losing commission. She had laughed at everything I said. "You sound tall," she had said over the phone. "Are you tall?"

"Not that tall," I said.

I was picturing her short, but when I met her a few days later, I was shocked to see that she was tiny, and her hair was red, and she had freckles and wore giant earrings. I sat across the table from her at T.G.I. Friday's, looking down at my plate of salmon and listening to her voice, trying to recall the image I'd had of her on the phone in my cubicle.

The girl who wanted tickets for Shakespeare was happy with what I'd done for her. She left it at that and hung up. The next six callers were happy too. I was happy for their happiness. I was the portal through which they must pass on their way to pleasure. I was the faceless voice on the end of the line that enabled them to have those memorable evenings, those exciting afternoons. If not for me, the little boys and girls of the city would never be able to see the clowns and elephants. They didn't know what I'd done for them, those little boys and girls, but I knew, and that was good enough for me.

By the tenth caller, I was bitter again. I was callous again. I knew I would be. My mouth was dry, my ears were buzzing. Plus I had to piss.

This is how my days go, *bringg, bringg; bringg, bringg,* every day pretty much the same as the day before: intimacy in intervals of three minutes or less—three minutes or less if you want to make enough commission—holding at bay my desire and antagonism, and also my boredom, and not a little regret. The only thing that made today different, that made it stand out from any of the days before, was that Wally was coming back.

*   *   *

We gathered in the conference room. I was late getting there. I made a point of being late by staying in the bathroom. By the time I walked in, he still hadn't arrived. This added to my aggravation.

Everyone else was there, one hundred people standing shoulder to shoulder, surrounded by an overblown display of congratulation. If you didn't know it was January, you would have thought it was the Fourth of July. There was an American-flag cake in the middle of the table, three feet long and three inches thick, there were red-white-and-blue plates and napkins, there were red-white-and-blue cans of Coke, there were little ninety-nine-cent American flags. Hanging on the walls were the red-white-and-blue handmade signs telling Wally what a good job he'd done.

Three of the girls came my way. Amber and Melissa and Tiffany.

"Here you go, hon," they said.

"Here you go, Zeke."

"Here's one for you."

They stuck an American-flag pin in my lapel. They touched me and leaned close.

"What I really want is a slice of that cake," I said suggestively.

"That's for later, hon."

They had French manicures, they had highlights, they smelled like apricots.

Twelve months ago, almost to the day, we'd clumped together in this same room, one hundred of us, saying goodbye to Wally. Everyone had cheered. Everyone had stomped their feet and chanted, "Wally, Wally! U.S.A.!" I'd done it too, despite myself. That is an example of how you can get caught up in the spirit of the moment.

About an hour after his going-away party, Wally had come into my cubicle and stood by my desk, close to my desk, playing with my paper clips and waiting for me to get off the phone. When I hung up, he said, "I just wanted to say, see you around sometime, Zeke." He had his mailbag slung over his shoulder, half filled with mail. He looked like a paperboy. I'd known him from the neighborhood when snot had dripped from his nose even in the summertime, when he'd been undersize and chubby and the teachers had thought he might be retarded. Everyone had made fun of him except for me. I'd had compassion for some reason. I'd been the one who had chased down two boys who'd been jabbing him in the belly with sticks. "Aw, we was just playing around." Those boys were bigger than me, but they cowered. By high school I had built a reputation for being fearless and exceptional. I'd been the one who had stood on-stage at graduation and told the other students what life held in store for them. "Give your best, get your best!" I'd said. The parents had loved that. But it was Wally, slow and runny Wally, who, on his own initiative, had gone down to the Career Center one morning before work and signed up for the army, and I was the one who sat at a desk all day long with a headset on.

So when he came into my cubicle to say goodbye, I said, without missing a beat, "I'm real proud of you." I tried to say it like I meant it, hoping he wouldn't detect that underneath was condescension, and underneath the condescension was jealousy, and after that lay melancholy.

The next thing I knew, he was sitting down on the floor, Wally was, sitting down between my cubicle wall and desk, wedging himself in as if playing hide-and-seek, hugging his mailbag to his chest with both arms and squeezing his knees up to his chin, all the while whispering something over and over, something that I had to lean down to hear, something about being scared, Zeke, about not wanting to go, Zeke.

"I don't want to die, Zeke," he nearly hyperventilated. He looked at me with baby-blue eyes that were filled with tears.

I stood up so fast that the wire from my headset caught around the arm of my swivel chair and yanked the headset off my head like a rubber band. "You're not going to die!" I said.

"Yes," he said, "I am." He said it like he knew it.

After that, I didn't know what to say. What I really wanted to do was jab him in the belly with a stick. Maybe he *was* going to die. Maybe this was what his whole life had been leading up to and he was going to be one of those unlucky soldiers who caught it, one of those few unlucky soldiers who never made it back out of the five hundred thousand who did. He'd come back in a coffin with the flag draped over the top. I'd go to his funeral. His dad would hug me and say, "Thank you for everything."

"You have a greater chance of dying in a car crash," I said. But Wally didn't want to hear about odds. He shook his head, his lips trembled, snot leaked out. I squatted down like an elementary school teacher would, hand on his knee, firm but consoling tone. "You're not going to die," I cooed. I mustered compassion from somewhere, and I must have said it with enough conviction that he appeared to believe me. A few moments later he rolled himself up off the floor, wiped his nose on his hand, wiped his hand on his pants, tucked his shirt into his pants.

I took him by the shoulders then, squarely, masculinely, and to lighten the mood a little, I said, "Go kick some ass, Wally!"

I had been right: he didn't die. In fact, he was reborn. Here he was, entering the conference room unscathed, smiling, blushing hard, his head buzzed, his face tanned, waving his hands in the air like he'd just been having the time of his life. One hundred people cheered him all at once, one hundred phone operators clapping and stomping until the room shook. "Wally, Wally!" they called, "Wally, Wally! U.S.A.!" Even the cleaning girls had stopped by, Maria and Olga, clapping, thanking him for everything he gave. I clapped too. I stomped my feet too. Because this is how you get caught up.

He was a changed man. You could see that right away. He was electric now. He was fluid.

"Where'd you go, Wally?" I thought as I pounded my hands. "What'd you see, huh?"

"I've been places, Zeke," his grin seemed to be saying to me. "I've done things."

He looked like he'd lost weight. That was what he'd done. He looked like he'd put on muscle too. His gut was gone and his jaw was hard and he didn't resemble a large baby boy anymore. If his nose was running, I couldn't tell. Apparently neither could the girls who were throwing their arms around his neck and kissing him, one after another, including Brittany, the prettiest of them all, the one I'd gone out with two years ago when the managing director had given me free tickets for a show that had come to town. We'd gone to Applebee's afterward, Brittany and I, and I'd told her, "Order whatever you want. It's on me," because I wanted her to know that this was a date, that I had designs on her. But for whatever reason, our outing never seemed to rise above coworkers with free tickets gossiping about the workplace, and I ended the night kissing her on the cheek.

Now she was kissing Wally on the cheek, damn close to his mouth, leaving her lipstick on his face, and when she was done, the next girl stepped in, and when all the girls were done, they moved back in a circle to give him some space to breathe, so he could compose himself amid all the attention, and he stood in the center of the conference room, as if under a spotlight, while we waited for him to say something profound about his experience. But of course he didn't know what to say, profound or otherwise. He looked around at a loss, lipstick all over his face, staring blankly at a roomful of people he had only ever delivered mail to.

It was the managing director who broke the silence by raising a plastic cup of soda, saying how he was happy to have Wally back, how Wally had sacrificed for us, how it was a shame that after everything he'd been through, he had to come home to such cold weather.

But Wally didn't look like he'd been through much of anything. He didn't have one scratch on him, as far as I could tell. He looked like he'd given little and gained a lot. As the managing director droned on, I contemplated how, if I ever went over there and came back with a tan and no scratch, I would be ashamed of myself. I would be embarrassed. I would make sure I got a scratch even if it meant I had to inflict it myself. And then I'd stand in this conference room, the way I had stood onstage at my high school graduation, and give a speech about country and family and friends. Society too. "It's *you* I want to thank," I'd say. That would bring the house down.

"You're going to be losing your tan," the managing director said in conclusion, and slapped Wally on the back. At that, the room laughed, clapping and shouting, with Wally standing in the middle of it like one of those things in a snow globe, with applause showering down around him.

"What'd you see, Wally?" I asked out loud. No one could hear me. "What'd you do, huh?"

For a moment our eyes met and he smiled at me.

"Why, I killed a man, Zeke. That's what I've done."

Then the applause stopped, it stopped all at once, because the break was over and it was time to get back to work. The phones were ringing.

The phones kept ringing and Wally's hair grew back. In February the temperature dropped to zero degrees. For three straight days it stayed at zero. Then it dropped below zero. The roads froze and the pipes burst and the circus was canceled. Whatever commission we had earned had to be returned. That was company policy.

We continued to get closer to catching their man. We even had him surrounded once, briefly, but he was wily and managed to elude us. Not to worry, we were getting closer. Any day now.

Other than that, not much changed.

Then one morning, toward the end of the month, I woke

as I always did to the sound of my alarm going off. It was six-forty-five. *Wrangg, wrangg; wrangg, wrangg,* the alarm went. The alarm could have been the telephone ringing in my cubicle. Lying in bed with my eyes closed and the covers pulled up around my chin, I listened to the winter sounds: the wind and the windows and the salt trucks. I tried to recall what my dreams had been from the night before, but as usual, they were fading—I could remember only symbols. Paperweights. Redwoods.

At 6:50 my snooze went off and I opened my eyes and stared at the ceiling for a while, following my upstairs neighbor's footsteps going back and forth.

At 6:55 I had no choice but to get out of bed and go into the kitchen and go into the bathroom and go back to the bedroom, where I wondered if the neighbors in the apartment beneath mine were staring up at their ceiling.

"What's the word today, buddy?" I asked the man on the corner selling newspapers.

The word today was not different than the word yesterday. The word was that it was seventy-eight degrees over there and it was minus two over here.

"What's the word today, Zeke?" my fellow commuters on the train asked me.

The word was that they had four hundred and twenty-six casualties and we had three.

Above my head were the same government advertisements, and outside my train window was the same frozen landscape, except for the American flags, which were blowing fast. We pulled into the station at 8:34, just like we always did. And just like we always did, we crowded through the train door, every man for himself, and raced up the stairs because we were cold and because we had snoozed too long and cut it too close.

In front of us were our office buildings all lit up, including mine, and which, in a few minutes, I would be entering and riding the elevator to the forty-eighth floor, the elevator that went almost as fast as the train, as if I were being transported somewhere urgent.

But today, when the crowd turned left, I turned right. I took the side street that led to the boulevard that led to the waterfront. I was going to be late for work, but that didn't matter. Years ago I had cut school with Wally and we had come down and hung out by the waterfront and taken off our shirts. He'd been flabby and I'd been muscular. It had been a strange feeling to be free when everyone else was captive, and I'd had the idea that this was what it meant to be an adult.

Now sheets of ice were floating on top of the river and the wind was coming off hard. I had to bend in half against the wind that went under my coat and around my suit and tie. I walked fast and my breath came out white. My fingers felt like they were burning in my gloves.

The sign was plainspoken and unadorned. CAREER CEN-TER, it said. There was an American flag in the window, the window was fogged. I pushed open the door and entered a room where a man sat at a desk. He was sitting cockeyed to the desk, because he wasn't cut out for office work. He was dressed in a uniform. His hat was off and his head was buzzed. On the wall behind him was a picture of young men with their arms around each other's shoulders.

He looked up at me. He put his pen down. He stood. He smiled. He said, "I'm proud of you, son."

Everyone was proud of me. That was the first big change. The guy I bought the newspaper from in the morning was proud of me. "Bring him back dead or alive," he said. That was the only thing he'd said in months. The commuters on the train were proud of me. So were my parents, including my dad. My landlord was proud of me. He said, "You won't be needing any weather-stripping where you're going." I said, "I sure won't," because I was giving up my apartment anyway. And everyone at work was proud of me. The managing director came over to congratulate me, to shake my hand and let me know what he thought of men like me, to let me know that my job would be there when I got back. Later on, Amber and Melissa and Tiffany stopped by, waving those little ninety-nine-cent American flags like they were at a parade. They said, "We get to have another party!" Brittany even came by. "Are you going to send me a postcard?" She made a pouting face like I'd been the one to break her heart once already. "You know I will," I said, winking. When the phone rang, I imagined that the people on the other end were proud of me, which helped me help them, each and every one of them, even the rude ones, even the dumb ones. I went out of my way to help them. I could feel myself transforming, morphing into someone new. My senses seemed to be heightening as I sat there in my swivel chair—sight, sound, empathy.

When Wally came by with the mailbag, he congratulated me and then said right away, "I'm wondering if you could do me a big favor, Zeke." Shifting from foot to foot, he asked me if I wouldn't mind putting in a good word for him with the managing director. It was all about him. "I can answer phones," he said. He made it sound like anyone could do my job.

"I'll put in a good word for you," I said, but I was done putting in good words.

I had five days to go, five days before I shipped out for basic training, and the joke around the office was that I had better ship out before the war ended. We were closing in on their man. He was in the forest for sure. Or the mountains. The joke was that I might not get my office party after all. "You might not even get a tan," the girls said.

I stayed up late, packing my stuff. There were boxes every-where, filled with clothes and dishes and mementos from all those extracurricular activities in high school that made the teachers hold me up as an example of someone who was "more than just a student." It was past midnight by the time I'd finished packing, but I was filled with energy. I took off my shirt. It was cold and the windows breathed, but I felt imper-vious. I dropped and did push-ups right there, right there on the kitchen floor, because I figured I might as well get started with basic training, might as well start getting back in shape. I hadn't done push-ups in years, but I was able to do eighteen, no problem. Ten thousand hours with a headset on my head and I still had muscles in my arms, or the potential for mus-cles. There were some muscles in my legs too, because I did twenty-eight jumping jacks, no problem, working up a sweat and wondering if my neighbors, at midnight, were trying to trace the path my footsteps were making on their ceiling. I wound up going to bed at three o'clock, dreaming symbolically, and waking before my clock went off.

But when I woke, it was to something unsettling: the previous day, we had sustained nine fatalities. We'd never had nine. We'd never even had seven. It's nothing, I told myself, tomorrow it'll be back to normal, tomorrow we'll continue the hunt. This was Tuesday.

Wednesday brought the news that we had lost nine more. The newspaper guy, his face crisscrossed with scarves, peered at me with concerned eyes. There was an article that day, front page, about one of our soldiers, twenty-four years old, who, in the middle of the forest, had become separated from his company while looking for potable water. In his confusion, he had wandered into a town where he was set upon by the locals. Stripping him of his flak jacket, they dragged him on the end of a rope through the streets before displaying him in the square. They were going to try him, they said. After they tried him, they were going to hang him. There was a photograph of the soldier. His face frightened and dehydrated. He looked apologetic, regretful. Staring at his photo on the train ride, I couldn't get past the fact that there had been no potable water.

Thursday the news was worse, the news was unbearable. The balance had somehow swung in the opposite direction: we were the ones being pursued. The war was going to last longer than we thought. Maybe till summer. Maybe till fall. The experts could not agree. We would persevere in the end, of course, but for now, we were fleeing and they were chasing. The reports came in randomly, if at all. At last count, they had twenty-two casualties and we had seventy-seven. In addition, two of our companies were unaccounted for, and there was news that a general had been shot in the face. Of the soldier who had been captured while searching for water in the forest, there was no news, there were more pressing things with which to concern ourselves. Water was the least of it.

At work, no one said anything. I made it easy for them by staying in my cubicle. The only person who came by was Wally. His hair had grown even longer than before he left. It was in shaggy fashionable curls. His hair was an affront. I didn't know whether he was coming to see if I had put in a good word for him. I made a point of staying on the phone with a customer who wanted ten tickets to the expo. "Yes, ma'am," I said. "I can do ten tickets for you, ma'am." He stood by my desk, hovering. I wanted him to witness my composure. I wanted him to witness my commission. When he left, I hung up because there was no one on the line.

That night I took my stuff to my parents' house. Sixteen boxes of stuff. My whole life in those boxes. It was freezing and my car wouldn't start. It rattled and coughed for a while, and then the engine caught. No one was out on the street. The only things on the street were the flags, blowing so hard they looked like they were going to fly away. They had lost their celebratory quality. They had lost their sense of unity. Now they were holding on for dear life.

"It's like you're moving back home, Zeke," my dad said when I arrived.

It wasn't like that at all. He was dressed in suspenders because he was a lawyer. My mom was dressed in an apron because she was a stay-at-home mom. My sister was dressed in torn jeans and purple eye shadow because she was a teenager.

I put the boxes in the cellar where my childhood toys were, my baseball card collection, my comic book collection, my coin collection. I'd been a hoarder as a child. Now I would learn to live with nothing.

"Stack them alongside the wall," my dad said, referring to the boxes. He wasn't going to give me a hand.

It was cold and clammy in the cellar. I thought about whether the barracks were going to be cold and clammy. That was something I could ask him. There were a lot of questions I could ask him. I thought about how, if I was killed, my mom and dad would have to come down to the cellar and sort through all my stuff, trying to figure out what to keep and what to throw out. I'd want them to do what we did with my grandmother's possessions. We didn't bother to look through any of it, we just loaded it all into a truck, mementos and everything, and gave it to Goodwill. My beer can collection, my stamp collection, give it all away.

At some point I realized that it wasn't going to be cold and clammy in the barracks because it was seventy-eight degrees where I was headed. This failed to hearten me.

My mom had cooked a special dinner. "Chicken with stuffing, extra stuffing," she said. That was my favorite, but I didn't have an appetite. I hadn't had an appetite in four days.

My dad said a prayer, "Dear Lord . . ." He said some things about the past and the future, generic things that could be interpreted in a number of different ways. "Amen," he said.

"Amen," we said.

"Dig in," he said.

I ate to be nice. I picked, really. Moving the chicken and

stuffing around on my plate, hoping somehow to diminish the portion so my mom's feelings wouldn't be hurt. I could hardly swallow. I drank plenty of water, though. Four glasses of water.

"You sure are thirsty," my sister said.

"Is the chicken too salty?" my mom wanted to know.

"It's just right," I said.

"It's more than *just right,*" my dad said. He was always correcting me.

My sister wanted to catch up on everything, including her special activities in school, especially for the war. Like writing letters to soldiers.

"Are you going to send me a postcard?" I said.

"You know I will," she said. I thought I might weep. But for her it was exciting. She told me about a soldier she'd been corresponding with. I half-listened. She ended by saying, "You're going on an adventure, Zeke!"

This was Thursday.

Friday the news was worse. We had stopped fleeing because there was nowhere left to flee. It was official: we were surrounded. All we could do was hope for the best and wait for reinforcements. Friday was also the day I had my office party.

I was late getting there because I didn't want to go. If it were up to me, I would have canceled. To cancel, however, would have been to exhibit my fear. Or despair. I hung out in the bathroom, not doing anything, just standing in front of the mirror, letting the water run over my hands and staring at myself, wondering what I was going to look like with my head shaved and a flak jacket on, wondering what I was going to look like dehydrated. I already looked gaunt and hungover. I didn't have far to go.

After a while, Wally opened the door. "I've been looking for you," he said. He was standing in the doorway with a sad face, like he knew the end was coming.

"Can't talk now, Wally!" I said, as if bursting with enthusiasm. "I have a party to get to!"

There were one hundred people waiting for me in the conference room, standing shoulder to shoulder. It was so quiet it could have been a vigil. All that was missing were the candles. To their credit, they had spared no expense: there was cake, there was soda, there were signs on the walls that the girls had spent the morning making, and which, through either oversight or intention, all said the same thing: GOOD LUCK, ZEKE! ZEKE, GOOD LUCK! WE WISH YOU LUCK!

Luck was the thing I needed now.

As I took my place among the refreshments and decorations, the silence of the room deepened in that uncomfortable way, like when an audience doesn't know if the play has ended. I was trying to look happy for the fun party, but I could feel my eyebrows raised unnaturally. I was sorry to have put the crowd through this. The crowd was sorry too. Two hundred sorry eyes staring at me.

Then the managing director began to clap, and the rest of the room took that as their cue to get going with false enthusiasm. They tried to applaud with the same gusto that they had applauded for Wally, but it sounded scattered and hopeless. No one was calling my name.

Somehow I summoned the energy to raise my hands above my head as if victorious, and basking in the acclaim of tepid applause, I yelled, "Let's eat cake!" That got everyone stomp-ing and shouting, no doubt out of relief that I was able to show some zest for life. The managing director handed me a slice of red-white-and-blue cake, the biggest slice, of course. I ate it off a red-white-and-blue plate. And when I was done, I ate another. This was my party. The men came to shake my hand, and the girls came to kiss me on the cheek. "See you in twelve months," they said optimistically. Brittany put one of those American-flag pins in my lapel. She leaned in close and touched me. "Good luck," she whispered.

At one o'clock everyone got back to work, and I went to my cubicle to pack up. I had imagined it would take me all day to get everything organized and sorted and thrown out. I'd been in that cubicle two years, after all. It took about fifteen minutes. There were some odds and ends, including a couple of photographs of me and my coworkers on bowling night, when one of the guys had taken the initiative to schedule some work outings, since "work shouldn't be all about work." Al-most everything else in my desk belonged to the company. I thought about stealing something, a keepsake, but that's not the kind of person I am. I sat down in my swivel chair one last time, aware suddenly of how soft it was and how well it swiv-eled. I was going to miss my chair. I was going to miss my desk and headset. My headset smelled vaguely of sweat from hav-ing been on top of my head for ten thousand hours. I put it to my face and inhaled. On Monday morning, bright and early, someone new would come, someone who didn't know me, someone who didn't know how good he had it. Maybe it would be Wally, after all. Maybe it would be Wally who would sit in my swivel chair, and thumb through the instruction packet, and shake hands with the managing director, and joke with Brittany about his new career. If they mentioned me, it'd be in the past tense. And at ten o'clock on the dot, my phone would ring, and Wally would put on my headset, and he would say for the very first time, "Good morning. My name is Wally. How may I help you today?"

I went out the side door with my bag of things so I wouldn't have to see anyone else for the last time and make them embarrassed. I took the elevator down to the eighteenth floor. On the eighteenth floor, I transferred to the freight elevator.

The elevator guy said, "I haven't seen you in a while." It'd been two years since I'd gotten promoted. There was graffiti about pussies all over the walls

"I've been on vacation," I said.

"Oh, yeah," he said. "Where'd you go?"

He thought I was serious. To him, only a couple of weeks had passed since he'd last seen me. That's how time moves when you're in an elevator.

The subbasement was the same as always, boiling hot, even in the dead of winter, and smelling like envelopes. There were sixteen hallways in the subbasement, and if you didn't know which way you were going, you could get lost and wander for an hour. I knew exactly where I was going. I found Wally in the bulk section, sitting on a crate while he sorted envelopes, big, little, medium. He didn't look up when I came over. He was busy with his work, busy tossing envelopes left or right. One, two, three, he worked. He had concentration. He had work ethic. He deserved to have a good word put in for him. I'd done this for three years. I used to go home each night and wash my hands with lemon juice to try to get the smell of envelope off them. It had felt like a miracle when I moved upstairs.

For a moment I thought I might pass out, because it was hot in the subbasement, and because I'd eaten a lot of cake, and also because I knew this was it, that my "adventure" was about to begin and there was a good chance I wouldn't be coming back. I tilted slightly, briefly, and imagined myself falling into the narrow space between the big envelopes and the small envelopes. It wouldn't be that bad, I thought, to fall into that space. It wouldn't be that bad to do this kind of work again.

I stood to the side waiting for him to notice me, and when he looked my way, he stood up quickly. I said, "I just wanted to say, see you around sometime, Wally."

He put down the envelope he was holding. He put his hands in his pockets. He took them out. His face was flushed from the stuffiness. This was probably what the barracks was going to feel like.

"Did the managing director ever talk to you?" I asked, as if there was a possibility.

Wally shook his head.

"That's a shame," I said, but I was relieved. And then I was sorry. "Well, it's not that bad down here," I said. I smiled, I chuckled. As if to prove my point, I picked up an envelope, weighed its heft, and tossed it into the medium pile. But before I knew what was happening, I was sputtering, teetering, grasping Wally's hand, and saying, "I don't want to die, Wally. I don't want to die."

Wally grabbed me to steady me. He put his arm around my waist. He let me lean straight into him. We stood there like that for a while in the hot basement with the sound of the fan whirring in the background, with me heaving against him.

I kept waiting to hear Wally offer some words of comfort, of consolation. I kept waiting for him to talk to me about percentages and odds. Instead, he took me by the shoulders, firmly, tightly, looked me straight in the eye, and I suppose to lighten the mood a little bit, he said, "Go kick some ass, Zeke!"

It was dawn. It was oddly warm for dawn. Twenty-five degrees, maybe.

I was supposed to catch the bus at the depot—that was the instruction. I fully intended to follow all instructions. At the depot, there were fifty guys like me milling around. No one looked at anyone. Half of us stood there smoking cigarettes. There was a sign that said NO SMOKING, but we knew the basic laws of the land didn't apply to us anymore. The rest of us slouched in the blue plastic seats, trying to stay awake. A tall man came and sat down next to me. He had a can of Coke that he kept tipping all the way back, as if trying to get out every drop. Enjoy that last drop, I thought. His Adam's apple bobbed. He said to me, "Do you know where we're going?"

"I have no idea," I said.

"We're going for training," someone said, someone who was eavesdropping. Privacy didn't apply to us anymore either. Soon we'd be showering together.

"No," the tall man said to the eavesdropper, "we're going

straight to the forest." He chuckled like this was something that could be funny.

When the bus pulled in, the headlights came at us like giant yellow eyeballs. It was a Greyhound bus with an LCD display on the front that said GOD BLESS AMERICA. The bus had been rented free of charge for the war effort so that not everything would have to fall on the taxpayers.

An officer appeared out of nowhere. His hat was on and his shoes were shined. It was clear he wasn't a man who had trouble with the early hours of the morning. "Line up and get on" was what he said.

We did as we were told. This is day one, I thought.

A fat man sat down next to me with headphones on. He was already out of breath and would most certainly die within days. They weren't picky anymore. They were taking anyone who wanted to be a soldier. The man bobbed his head to whatever music was on his headphones, and when I looked at him, he pulled one of the headphones off of his ear and said confidentially, "If you've got music, you better listen to it now, because they're going to take it."

"Is that so?" I said.

"That is so," he said.

I wasn't going in for rumors. I wasn't going in for hysteria. I'd stay above the fray, the paranoia. I wanted cold hard facts. Cold hard facts were going to save me in the end. Facts and luck.

The officer came through the bus, doing a head count. His gun was on his hip. When he walked past me, the gun was at eye level.

Someone in the front shouted, "When am I going to get me one of those guns, Captain?" Everyone laughed.

The bus started, and we pulled out so smoothly. The bus hummed. We made a left and another left. I leaned back in my seat and found comfort in the swaying. Then I drifted off to sleep. But I didn't dream. And when I woke, we had arrived.

VICTORY

The story began to change for me the summer I was working at the supermarket in Montour Heights—that enormous state-of-the-art supermarket that had been built to great acclaim, with its forty-eight aisles, its ice cream parlor, its travel agency.

It was summer, but it was starting to get unseasonably cool, strangely cool, sixty degrees, fifty degrees sometimes. The days were overcast and the nights were chilly and when I left home in the morning there'd be frost on the leaves. The public pools had shut down and the price of heating oil had gone up and families picnicked in their living rooms in front of the television. It wasn't unusual to see people on the street dressed in corduroys and sweaters and sometimes gloves and hats. In the evening there'd be smoke coming out of the chimneys. No one cared about the weather, though, because everyone's attention was on the war. We'd taken the bay, we'd secured the border, and we'd had almost no casualties. Within a week we'd made it within fifty miles of the capital, and a week later we had closed to twenty-five, and it was agreed upon by all the experts, patriots and naysayers alike, that the enemy no longer stood a chance and now was the time to begin discussing the terms of settlement.

At the supermarket, business was booming. The factories had opened back up along the river like old times, and people had come in from the outskirts to work, and people needed to eat. Before and after our shifts, we would crowd into the break room—the cashiers, the baggers, the stock clerks, the butchers, the bakers, the man who collected the shopping carts— and talk about what was happening and what was going to happen. Fifty of us standing shoulder to shoulder in that windowless room, laughing and joking and breathing a sigh of relief because now that the end was near, it was evident there wouldn't be a draft. Some of the guys said they were thinking about enlisting anyway, before it was too late, so they could have an adventure. I said I was thinking about enlisting too, which made everyone laugh, because of course I would never be eligible. That summer everyone was happy and everyone was carefree. But then toward the middle of August, things started to bog down due to terrain and logistics, and for a while we advanced no more than a quarter of a mile a day, sometimes not even that, sometimes we lost ground, little by little we lost ground, until before long we were once again fifty miles from the capital. So after that we talked about other things.

In September Ziggy caught a girl shoplifting. I saw her first when I was coming through the produce aisle with my broom. Her back was to me, and she had long wavy hair that was the color of chocolate, and she had a nice ass, and she was eating strawberries straight out of the bin as if she owned the place. No regard. It was about four o'clock and I was late on my tasks because I'm overworked, but I lingered, hoping I might have an opportunity to chat her up, which is what I imagine whenever I see a pretty girl—imagine but never undertake. I wasted some time sweeping up the stray lettuce leaves, even the ones that had been ground into the floor, which I generally leave for the guy on night turn. My good side was facing her way, so that if she happened to turn around, I would be at my most handsome and appealing, and I would say something in the nature of "What's your name?" and she would blush and tell me and we would go from there. When she did turn around, however, I saw that her face was covered with acne, like sunburn, painful no doubt, red and splotchy and concentrated around her forehead and cheeks but also her chin and nose. She was staring at me as if about to ask a question, one side of her mouth puffing out like a chipmunk's because of the strawberry in her mouth. I wanted to look away out of respect. I could detect that underneath the acne she was a very pretty woman, with brown eyes and high cheekbones and puffy lips that were noticeably without blemish. She was wearing a fur coat with an American-flag pin on the collar, and below the pin were her breasts. I knelt down to gather up the pile of lettuce leaves and when I stood up, she was gone.

That could have been the end if I hadn't run into her again, not over twenty minutes later, as I was wheeling my trash bin past the row of hot soups. This time she was putting a plastic spoonful of clam chowder into her mouth, tasting it slowly and making a big show of considering its merits before moving on to the next selection. She was trying to appear as if she were having a small sample of each before deciding which one to purchase, but it was clear that she was one of those people who intended to eat an entire meal within the confines of the supermarket. I didn't appreciate this, because I'm a company man at heart, but she was a poor girl—I could tell that now—and since I have my own struggles, I felt some affinity for her. She was doing her best to conceal the reality of her condition, but I've learned well that the unforgiving fluorescent lights of the supermarket eventually reveal all, and seeing her poised above the steaming pots of soup, I noticed that her long chocolate hair was unwashed and unkempt, and her fuzzy coat had tufts missing from the collar and wrists.

Coming down the aisle was Ziggy, pushing his shopping cart filled with two weeks' worth of groceries. He wasn't a customer. He was an undercover, and today he was dressed like a soldier in camouflage and combat boots. Yesterday he'd been a construction worker wearing a hard hat and tool belt. Tomorrow he might come dressed as a baseball player or whatever other profession struck his fancy. Halloween was two months away, but for him every day was Halloween. "Why don't you come one day dressed as an undercover?" I joked with him once.

"Because I'd give myself away," he had responded solemnly. He was slow like that sometimes.

He winked at me as we passed each other. He knew what the girl was up to, and he knew that I knew. He loved this. He lived for this. I'd known him since middle school, where he had developed a passion for tattling. He once tattled on a girl for copying off his math test, even though it was no skin off his back. Her parents had to be brought in for a conference. Things like that can mar you for life. Now he earned twice as much as I did, and he didn't do anything but spend his day strolling up and down the forty-eight aisles, gazing at the assortment of products, studying, pondering, selecting, then handing me his shopping cart at the end of his shift so I could return every single item to the shelves. Most days he was just an endless shopper full of suspicion of other shoppers, hoping for his intuition to be proved right to affirm him and release him from his tyranny of wandering. His original dream was to be a cop, but like a lot of people's dreams, this one was dashed, mainly because he failed the written exam three times. "They're all idiots anyway," he told anyone who would listen, near tears, inverting the judgment. He was thinking about joining the army now. Once the war ended, of course. Or the marines. He was chubby and easily winded, but I supposed he had a shot. "Keep striving for your goal," I encouraged him. It was what my father always said when he found himself at a loss for what to tell me next.

Ziggy passed me as I passed her. She had moved on to sampling the broccoli soup. I wanted to hang around long enough to see the exciting moment of revelation when the soldier takes his true form and removes his store ID, but the loudspeaker clicked on just above my head, and Mr. Moskowitz, as if he were a fire captain ordering his men into the burning building, screamed with great urgency, "There's a cleanup in aisle thirty-nine!" So I had to wheel my trash bin around and return the way I had come, through the maze of aisles, past the cheese court and the chocolate confectioner and the ice cream parlor, to the back room, where I retrieved my mop and bucket from the mop and bucket closet, then hurried all the way to aisle thirty-nine, where someone, through negligence or spite, had knocked over a display of molasses. A half-dozen bottles lay smashed in the middle of the floor, and from them oozed a great puddle that was widening slowly, almost imperceptibly, oozing across the aisle as if it were a lake at the beginning of time that, if left long enough, would engulf the entire supermarket.

No, I don't have a problem cleaning: I hold the mop in my good hand and the crook of my bad arm, and I swing it like a normal person, and when I need to rinse it out, I dip it in the bucket, keeping it tight against my chest as if I'm dancing close, and I wring it out with my good hand, and that could also be just like a normal person.

Midway through my endeavor, three cashiers walked by on their way to the break room. "Hiiiiiiiiiiiiiiiii, Max," they said. Sabrina and Jessica and Melanie. They wore fake nails. They wore eye shadow. They chewed gum.

"Hiya," I said, and I paused to watch them sashay their way down the aisle.

After that, Pink from coffee came past, high on pot and wired on caffeine, wearing his giant watch that glinted in the fluorescent light. I was waiting for him to get fired so I could take his job. How hard is it, really, to pour a cup of coffee?

He said rapid-fire, "Working hard or hardly working?" Which is what he says almost every time.

"Workingly hard," I responded.

He never stopped thinking this was hilarious, and he

laughed in slow motion, bending in two and propelling himself forward as if ascending a mountain.

And then Howie from deli came past. I could smell him before I saw him. He reeked of salami and cologne, the latter of which he used in an attempt to camouflage the former. He wasn't much older than me, but he acted like an elderly man, joyless and embittered, whose best days were behind him, which they probably were. He slouched noticeably to his right, almost like a hunchback, because he spent eight hours a day slicing four-pound blocks of meats and cheeses. I'd switch jobs with him any day too. He didn't look up when he walked by. He said without any trace of humor, "What'd you do, Max, huh, take a shit on the floor?"

When the customers came by, they were all smiles, real sweet smiles, real sympathetic smiles, and they stepped lightly and took an extra-wide berth to show their consideration and compassion.

"You're an inspiration, Max," they'd say, addressing me by way of my name tag.

At one point, a husband and wife arrived with two shopping carts and five children, three of whom wanted to play in the puddle of molasses. The other two stared at me while they aimlessly waved small American flags that were being sold at the front of the store for ninety-nine cents. While the wife was trying to corral the younger ones, the husband took the time to tell me that I was living proof that if people really wanted a job, they could have one.

"There's good and bad in all people," he said.

"You got that right," I said.

"That's why we're in this mess today," he said, meaning the war and meaning society. He was getting worked up and wanted to keep talking about the guys he knew who were over there fighting, and the guys he knew who were over here doing nothing. I would have let him keep talking, but his wife said they should go so I could get back to work.

Before she left, she leaned in close, discreetly, and said as if telling me a secret, "You're one of God's angels, Max."

When I got back to the back room, justice was running its course. The girl with the acne was sitting on top of a giant cardboard box filled with containers of laundry detergent. One of her wrists was handcuffed to the steam pipe that ran two hundred feet to the ceiling, and she was rocking back and forth, explaining how it was a big misunderstanding. They all said it was a big misunderstanding after they'd been caught. I once watched a man try to claim he had no idea there were eight packs of cigarettes down his pants.

"You don't understand!" the girl gasped.

The day's delivery hadn't come in yet, and the back room was empty, like a stadium before a game. In the vacant space, the girl's cries were amplified and her size diminished. Ziggy was unmoved. He was all business, oblivious to her beseeching. He was in the process of pulling things out of her fur coat like a magician: cookies and lipstick, chips and cheese, it was endless. He didn't care about the strawberries or soup in her stomach. They were the least of it. When he was satisfied that he had bested her sleight of hand with his own sleight of hand, he snapped open his briefcase with authority, showing how wrong the police force had been for passing him over three times.

On the wall behind the girl's head was an array of photographs, almost like a memorial, of the people who had been apprehended over the years, with name and age, staring out at the camera with their bounty held in front of them, their shame lasting into eternity. Once caught, they could never return to the supermarket, but I had become so familiar with their faces that it was as if they shopped there every day. Children with candy, moms with milk, men with meat. To this collection of hundreds of unhappy faces, sullen, grim, imploring, occasionally smirking faces, would soon be added the girl's face. As I put away the mop and bucket, her voice echoed behind me.

"You, you, you, don't, don't, don't, understand . . ."

And then Ziggy responded with his own plaintive call for help: "My forms!"

His face was red and anguished, embarrassed and humiliated, as if he had been the one caught cheating on the spelling test. He held up his empty briefcase, showing how right the police were for passing him over. "Goddammit, Ziggy!" he scolded himself in the third person, and he kicked his way through the swinging doors with his combat boots, Lieutenant Ziggy en route to procure the necessary paperwork. The doors banged back and forth six times before coming to rest.

Soon the day's delivery would arrive, three hundred pallets of groceries—double the amount since the factories reopened—to be unloaded from the eighteen-wheeler by the night turn manager, Tom or Tim, depending. Among my many tasks, it was my responsibility to make sure the loading dock was clear and accessible, so that nothing would be in Tim or Tom's way when he got to work, so that nothing would slow him down, since the drivers made forty dollars an hour—and I made eight—and the manager had to get them back on the road as soon as possible. Every once in a while I would ask Tom or Tim if he might consider putting in a good word for me with Mr. Moskowitz about the possibility of becoming a stock clerk. How hard is it, really, to put cans on a shelf? But they'd hem and haw and make up some excuse about how the time wasn't right, Max, about how they'd see about it later, sometime later, about how I should remind them about it later. I'd heard it all before. In the meantime, they'd say, "Time is money, Max. Let's keep the loading dock clear."

I pushed the green button and the gate churned upward, letting daylight into the back room and the smell of the factory smoke coming from along the river. It smelled like melting plastic. There was also a breeze, coming unimpeded through the parking lot, reminding everyone that winter was going to be early this year, that winter was going to be bad. Sitting on the dock were some saggy bags of garbage, filled and leaking, alongside a cart piled with cans and bottles, dropped off by concerned customers, and which needed to be sorted and recycled. I placed the bags of garbage in the cart and wheeled it inside, and then I threw everything down the garbage chute, every single can and bottle and bag of trash, because I have too much to do and I don't have time to sort and recycle.

When I turned around, I saw that the girl was staring at me. She was quiet and had stopped rocking back and forth.

She seemed resigned to her fate. Her hand, held aloft on the steam pipe by the handcuff, made her appear to be in the process of trying to hail a taxi. I tried not to look at her because it's embarrassing to be free when someone else is captive, but in the dim daylight of the back room, her face was very pretty, her acne less acute, and her chocolate hair had regained its luster. I moved awkwardly, self-consciously, trying to keep my good side facing her way, although it was most likely too late for that. She had discovered what everyone eventually discovers, that my left arm is considerably smaller than my right, about half the length. I make sure to always wear a three-quarter sleeve to save everyone the predicament of having to see my arm twisted like a corkscrew and topped by a withered and nearly useless hand, three fingers only, no thumb, more fish fin than human limb, and which I can use to do things like unscrew the cap on a bottle, but that's about it. "We all have our burdens to bear," my minister had told me years ago when I was about twelve years old, taking me aside one Sunday after service and quoting at length some scripture that he said applied directly to my situation, and which I felt emboldened by at the time but can no longer recall.

Looking out at me from the great tableau of faces on the wall above the girl's head was one in particular, that of a young boy, redheaded and freckled. In the photograph, he is holding a bag of pretzels in front of his chest as if it's a prize he's won, and he is smiling at the camera because he isn't quite sure what's happening and because he was taught to smile whenever he has his picture taken. He was apprehended years ago and would be a man by now, maybe older than I am, but he has been preserved forever in that photograph at age ten.

No matter what he goes on to accomplish in his life, he will never outlive this crime.

I happen to know that hidden behind the photograph is a spare key, and it was that key I used to unlock the girl's wrist from the steam pipe. She yielded with a whimper. Her wrist was pliant and thin. I led her to the loading dock and I clicked the red button so that the gate began to churn down. Then I let her go, releasing her the way trainers release birds back into the wild. She ducked beneath the closing gate without hesitation and without thanks. The last things I saw were her feet.

I spent the rest of my shift avoiding Ziggy. It wasn't that hard. I'd catch sight of him in the aisles and head the other way. It slowed me down but I got most of my work done. I finally ran into him in the break room, where he was eating a bag of chips like a pig, leaving crumbs all over the floor—perhaps as an act of revenge. He looked at me glumly, sitting there in his fatigues, but all he said was "It's snowing."

It had never snowed in September. It hardly ever snowed in October. When I exited the supermarket, the flakes were fluttering in the parking lot lights as if suspended on invisible wires. It was nine o'clock at night, but customers were still coming. They pushed past me as if they were trying to get into a rock concert with shopping carts. Two hours later they'd be pushing their carts the other way, filled with five hundred dollars' worth of groceries. Next week they'd do it again. My main concern was that they would be tracking snow across my floor.

A couple of the stock clerks were getting off at the same time and they stopped to watch the flakes with me. So did the guy who scoops ice cream in the ice cream parlor. So did the travel agent. So did some of the cashiers. Night turn was just coming in and they stood along with everyone else. It was like we were watching fireworks in July.

Howie from deli stopped too. He smelled like bologna and deodorant. "If it's snowing in September," he said, "what's it going to be like in January?" He ruined the moment. We all got in our cars and drove home.

The next morning the sun was out but there were eight inches on the ground. School was canceled and children from the neighborhood had assembled in the street to have a snowball fight. I sat in my kitchen and watched them play: they were fearless and they were ruthless, and they hit each other in the face. Half were the Americans and half were the enemy. "Kill, kill, kill," they screamed. The snow made everything in the neighborhood look white and clean and newly restored, like in the photographs from fifty years ago when times were good. Before I got in the shower, I opened the window and gathered snow off the windowsill and made a snowball about the size of a cantaloupe. It took me a little longer than the average person, but I got it done. "Here comes the atom bomb," I yelled, and the boys and girls looked up at me with terror and delight as I hurled it down on their heads.

They said, "Do it again, Max! Do it again!"

"But you're all dead," I said.

"Do it again!"

I had to get to work.

Since we were an important city, a vital city, the mayor had sent trucks round-the-clock to clear the roads, and I had no trouble making it to the supermarket on time. Nearly every-body else was late. There were five cashiers when there should have been nine, and there were three baggers, and there was no one in dairy, and the flag displays were all empty. The manag-ers ran back and forth like fools, trying to figure out what to do next.

In the locker room, Pink from coffee was slowly changing into his uniform. It was nine o'clock and he was already high. How he'd made it to work on time, I had no idea.

"Check out my watch," he said. He displayed his wrist. He always had a new watch, always larger the last one. This one had a gold face with diamonds around the edge. You could tell the time from a block away.

"That sure is a nice fake watch," I said.

"I can get you one," he said. He looked at me significantly.

"No, thanks," I said. "I don't need to tell time."

He thought this was funny. He laughed hard but with no sound. Two late baggers sauntered in as if they were on their way to a day at the beach, and I wanted to tell them that I'd take their job any day. How hard is it, really, to place objects into a bag?

When I took off my shirt, everyone looked away.

"Check out my watch," Pink said to the baggers.

Mr. Moskowitz had the door to his office wide open, and as I was coming out of the locker room, he called out to me like a general ordering his soldier to the front line. "Max!" he said. He sounded angry, he sounded exhausted. Everything that came out of his mouth sounded angry or exhausted. The day he hired me, he sighed, leaned far back in his swivel chair like he was about to fall asleep, and said, "I guess I'll take a chance on you." I wanted to tell him, "Don't do me any favors, pal." I wanted to tell him that I knew he was getting a tax break for hiring me. Instead I said, "Thank you, sir. You won't be sorry, sir." Because the truth was, I needed all the favors I could get. "You don't need to call me *sir*," he said.

This morning he was halfway through a Hostess cupcake, presumably his breakfast. His belly was pressed against the desk, which was littered with spreadsheets of facts and figures—the lifeblood of the supermarket. He worked six to six, he worked six days a week, he'd been here twenty years. He'd be here another twenty years, then he'd retire and move to the suburbs. On the wall behind him was his framed diploma from college, and next to it was a recruiting poster that showed a group of smiling models dressed like stock clerks and cashiers, standing with their arms around each other's shoulders, above a caption that read, WE OFFER FREE DENTAL EXAMS.

He was staring at me hard from behind his desk. Angry and exhausted. Suspicious too. Also disappointed. He didn't take his eyes off me. His stare chilled me. I understood suddenly why I was being summoned. Namely the girl from the day before. Ziggy had ratted me out after all—just like the poor little girl with the math test. What could I say? I had breached the company's trust, maybe even committed a felony. And here I was, a company man at heart. It was too late to make amends now. The supermarket had taken a chance on me and I had repaid it with dishonesty. "If you give one hundred percent," my schoolteachers had told me years ago, "you get one hundred percent right back." It was a phrase I had heard often, and it returned to me with the full force of its haunting implication: *you get what you deserve.*

"You wanted something, Mr. M.?" I said. I tried my best for playful informality.

He was having none of it. "I was about to page you," he said. He leaned away from his desk as if about to stand. Instead he sat deeper. He was perspiring in his wash-and-wear suit despite the weather. The exchange was not going to take long. He'd have me packed and ready to go by the time he finished eating his cupcake. I once watched him tell a cashier of fifteen years, "You must gather your things, leave, and never come back." That had been that.

His gaze bore into me.

"The faggots from the city blocked my car in," he said. "Do me a favor."

No, I don't have a problem shoveling. I hold the shovel in my good hand and the crook of my bad arm. Ten minutes in, I hadn't been able to make much progress. The car looked like it had been wrapped in marshmallow, but the snow was packed hard like concrete. I chipped away at it, making small piles. Then I moved the small piles into big piles. *Chink, chink, chink,* went my shovel. The air was cold but clear, and every so often I would catch a faint whiff of the smoke coming off the factories. It smelled like bug spray. After ten minutes, I broke through to Mr. Moskowitz's back bumper, where there was a red-white-and-blue bumper sticker that said HOLD STEADY.

The man who collected the shopping carts rolled by with a

train of fifteen. "That's not in your job description," he said. He was a union man from way back.

"It's in my job description now," I said.

He rolled on.

Cars were beginning to fill up the parking lot, a long line of cars coming to load up with boxes and bottles, cans and bags, coming to eat and digest and excrete. Over by the loading dock, I could see a woman waving to me. I'm always happy to help customers load their groceries, and I'm also always happy to accept a gratuity, even though supermarket policy prohibits accepting gratuities. And when they see my arm, they are inclined to be extra generous. Toward the far end of the parking lot I walked, with my shovel resting on my shoulder like a miner, and as I got closer I saw that this particular woman didn't have a shopping cart, in fact, didn't have any groceries. What she had was long brown hair, and a coat with fur missing from the collar, and a face that was covered with acne.

"Do you remember me?" she said as if our interaction had happened a year ago. She smiled. She was chewing gum and it had turned her lips a shade of purple.

I didn't know what to say. So I said, "I don't think so," because under the circumstances I thought it in my best interest to feign ignorance. For all I knew, Mr. Moskowitz was about to come around the corner at any moment. Followed by Ziggy. Followed by the district manager who stops in once every six months.

She seemed surprised by my response. She had no response for my response. She stood on the opposite side of a foot-high railing where the jitney drivers have to wait, as if she feared that merely stepping onto supermarket property would be grounds for her arrest—which it might very well have been. I got the sense that she had rehearsed something to say but I had confounded her by veering from the script. Now she was onstage, at a loss for what to say or do next. In lieu of dialogue, she blew a purple bubble.

I tried to think of something to say myself, something that might be appropriate at a time like this, but the best I could conjure was "Do you need help with your groceries?" There were no groceries, of course.

She smiled at me, more of an embarrassed smile. Her teeth were very white and very straight; they stood in contrast to her imperfect face. I wondered if the cold air helped or hurt her skin. I wondered if she'd stolen the gum she was chewing.

Then she snickered to herself and announced, "See you around sometime, Max." The sound of my name in her mouth was electric. She turned and walked through the parking lot entrance where the cars were entering; she walked quickly and disappeared around the corner.

The moment she was out of sight, I stepped over the railing and ran. I ran with my shovel. No, I don't have a problem running.

It was underneath the neon sign that proclaimed NOW OPEN 24 HOURS! that I caught up to her. She whirled around. Her eyes were wide.

"What's your name?" I said.

Her name was Amanda, and she was twenty-two years old, and she wasn't a poor girl at all. She was a very rich girl. She lived in Amberson Valley, where I'd never been, because you have no business being in Amberson Valley unless you live there. Her house was set back from the road, at the end of a long driveway, and hidden behind some big trees with a hammock strung between them that was filled with snow.

"We're not rich," she said, "we're comfortable."

"Whatever you want to call it," I said.

Her parents were both professionals doing something or other, investing and psychiatry I think it was, and her little brother was ten years old and already talking about college. They had paintings on the walls, they had a library, they had a skylight, and the first time she brought me home, she took me down to the basement to give me a tour of the wine cellar.

"This is from France," she said. "This is from Spain. This is only for special occasions. This is for Christmas." Then she stopped talking about wine and put her arms around my neck and pressed me up against the bottles. I was anxious, mainly about breaking something expensive but also about my bad arm. I hadn't kissed anyone since eighth grade, when I'd danced with a girl in the school gym.

Before it could go any further, her little brother screamed down into the basement, wanting to know what we were doing, wanting to know if he could come down.

"Shut the fuck up!" Amanda screamed back.

Then her father screamed down into the basement, "Don't use that language in my house!"

At dinner, we sat on opposite sides of the table, Amanda and I, our feet touching underneath. Before eating, we bowed our heads while her father said a prayer, a long meandering prayer about new friendship and good company.

"Amen," we said.

Her mom said, "This wine is from Savoy, Max."

We made small talk about the snow, about the war, about the wine, about whether or not there was going to be a draft.

"What does the future hold in store for you, Max?" her father asked me.

It was a legitimate question, but it put me on the spot. He put down his fork and waited. His wife waited too. They were going to wait as long as they needed. The table was silent. From the moment I entered the house, I'd been sure I was going to say or do the wrong thing. Or break something. Now, with all eyes on me, I had no idea what to answer about the general trajectory of my future. Meanwhile, Amanda was rubbing her foot up my leg.

"If I give one hundred percent," I said, trying to affect some expertise, "I get one hundred percent back."

Amanda's father looked at me as if he'd never heard anything like that before. "I think there's some real truth to that, Max."

"I think so too," Amanda's mother said.

Amanda's brother took it as an opening to list all of his activities. "I'm on the debate team. I'm on the tennis team. I'm on the Monopoly team." He sounded like he was going to grow up to be a real asshole.

Midway through the meal, Amanda had to take her acne medicine. Everyone got quiet as she took out the bottles and shook the pills into her palm one by one, big colorful pills, pills for a horse. She swallowed them with a tall glass of water.

Her mother said, "I think I'm beginning to see a change,

honey," and her father said, "I think so too," and her little brother said, "I'm not seeing any change."

"Shut the fuck up, Oscar!" Amanda said.

She was a thief. That had already been established. The only surprise was that she admitted it so openly.

"I'm a kleptomaniac," she told me. She wasn't proud, but she wasn't particularly ashamed. "It's a phase." She shrugged.

"How long does this phase last?" I asked.

She didn't know.

She was a thief and she was about to finish college. "I want to help the world," she said.

On our first real date, I took her ice-skating at the rink at the mall by the river. They'd decided to open the rink early this year. If it was so cold, you might as well make use of the cold.

COME IN FROM THE COLD, the sign read, which was a joke, because the rink was outdoors.

At the entrance, Amanda wanted to see if we could forgo the admission and get in for free by sneaking past the guard who was barely paying attention. "Please, please, please," she said. "I want to, I want to, I want to." The compulsion was laid bare. Her eyes were intense but also blank.

"Sneaking past a guard," I said, "doesn't count as klepto-mania." That seemed to put her at ease, and she let me pay the full price.

The rink was crowded with people, half of whom I knew. "Maaaaaaaaaax," they called out when they saw me. Amanda and I went around in a circle, her hand in my good hand, taking our time. "You're so sweet, Max," she said, and she put her head on my shoulder. I could smell her shampoo and I could smell the factories burning.

It turned out she was a good skater, but I was better. I would have been a hockey player if the story had been different for me. I would have been a lot of things.

Around and around we skated, without variation, like a merry-go-round. It was trancelike. "Look at the time, Max," Amanda said, and we saw that it was late, that it was night, that it was past dinnertime.

So we went to Burger King, where I knew the guy who worked the register, a guy named Mordecai from high school. He'd been at Burger King six years and had a brother in the military. When he handed me my order, there were extra fries on the tray. He winked.

"Tell your brother I said hi?" I said.

"My brother?" he said. His eyes dropped. "He's dead, Max. You didn't hear?"

I said, "I sure am sorry to hear that, Mordecai."

"Come on, man." He laughed. "My brother just got promoted to lieutenant!"

As we sat at the table, stuffing our faces, Amanda said, "Do eating these extra fries count as shoplifting?" She had a point.

I didn't live that far away from Burger King, so I brought her over to my apartment. "Just to stop by for a second." I wanted it to seem casual, like an afterthought. Meanwhile, I was wondering if I could get her undressed.

I gave her a grand tour of the apartment. "This here is from Walmart," I said, "this here is from Kmart."

There was fake wood paneling and green carpeting and the smell of cigarette smoke from the neighbor below. The green carpeting was in every room, including the bathroom.

"I'm planning to put down new carpeting," I said.

"Your house has charm," she said. She thought everything had charm. She thought Burger King had charm. She thought the supermarket had charm. She thought I had charm.

We made out on the couch. The couch that I'd gotten from Walmart. I put my good hand straight up her sweater and she didn't resist. Her stomach was smooth. Her bra was smooth. Her breasts were smooth. I thought about doing things with her, things I'd seen in videos, a number of which were hidden under the very couch we were sitting on. She must have been thinking things too, because she tried to pull my shirt straight over my head in one motion. That put an end to the proceedings. I pulled away and tucked my shirt back in. "I have to work in the morning" was what I said.

I drove her back home over the bridge. We had a good view of the factories all lit up.

"I should get a job down there," I said.

"Like doing what?" she said.

"Like stoking the furnaces," I said. What did I care? I pictured myself wearing overalls and a hard hat.

"You think you can stoke furnaces, Max?" she said.

"I can do whatever I set my mind to," I said.

She didn't say anything for a while. Then she said, "You'd be back at the supermarket in a week, begging to mop floors again."

She was probably right.

She clicked open the visor and examined her face in the

mirror. She took out a tube of lotion and put some on, rubbing it in small deliberate circles, clockwise and then counterclockwise. It smelled like lavender. I wondered if she'd stolen it. She used all sorts of lotions and potions, each one the one that was going to be the miracle cure.

"I think I'm beginning to see a change," she said.

"I think so too," I said.

"Really?" she said.

But I wasn't so sure.

When I got to her house, she kissed me hard on the mouth. Then she reached in her pocket and handed me ten packets of ketchup that she'd taken from Burger King.

I said, "You know those are free, right?"

She got out of the car and her brother came out on the porch. He was holding a snowboard. "I'm on the snowboarding team," he said.

When I got back home, I checked to see if she'd stolen anything. I checked everywhere, kitchen, bathroom, dresser drawers. I couldn't find anything missing.

Halloween was coming. The days passed. The temperature rose. The snow melted and turned to slush. Everyone who had complained about the snow now complained about the slush. When the slush finally disappeared down the sewers, everyone complained about the cold. It was only October and it was going to be a winter full of complaint.

The war continued to hold steady, and we continued to lose ten to fifteen men a day, which wasn't that many, all things considered. The experts said you had a better chance of dying in a swimming pool than dying in a war. The bodies came home in coffins draped with flags, as we held steady. Driving home at night, I'd pass the Halloween displays in front of the stores and homes. They were exceptionally imaginative and gruesome this year—bodies impaled, bodies decapitated, bodies on fire, along with the conventional artifacts of unease: pitchforks and black cats and spiderwebs. By late October, we were losing twenty-five men a day, which still wasn't that many.

At the supermarket, business continued to boom. The deliveries increased to three a week and then four. In the afternoon, there'd be a line of eighteen-wheelers pulled up to the loading dock like cattle at the trough. Mr. Moskowitz ordered the guys on night turn to come in two hours earlier, but even that wasn't good enough, even with Tom and Tim shouting like drill sergeants. In the morning, the back room would be filled with pallets of every kind of food imaginable, stacked floor to ceiling, so that I had to push my mop and bucket through narrow paths as if I were a mouse in a maze of cardboard skyscrapers. Everyone was trying to cut corners, trying to do things faster, including the stock clerks, who got into the habit of pulling their boxes out from the bottommost pallet and undermining the foundation, so that one afternoon, about thirty minutes before I was supposed to punch out, an entire skyscraper of produce collapsed. It sounded like an explosion when it fell. Two hundred pumpkins lay crushed on the floor like bodies in a disaster. I was the one who had to clean them up. I had to use two mops and a shovel. This time when Pink from coffee came past, he didn't bother to make his usual joke about hardly working. His big fake watch told him he had five minutes left for his break. "Hardly hard?" I called after him. He didn't think it was funny. Howie from deli walked by, reeking of aftershave and cheese and saying somberly, "I wish that was my head on the floor." The cashiers passed, not saying hiiiiiiiiiiiiiiii, because they were working double shifts, and so were the butchers, and the bakers, and the baggers, and so was the man who collected the shopping carts in the parking lot whose hands were red from the cold. "That's a safety violation" was what he said when he saw the mess. The only person who wasn't having a problem with the workload was Ziggy, who was catching an average of three shoplifters a day and having the time of his life posting new photographs on the wall in the back room.

But on Halloween things changed for the better: we were on the move again, making progress toward the capital. That day, every thirty minutes, Mr. Moskowitz would click on the loudspeaker and announce, "Forty miles to go!" He'd shout like he was calling bingo. "Thirty-nine miles to go!" A great and spontaneous cry would rise up across the forty-eight aisles, people shouting and screaming, customers and employees alike. Everyone was happy and everyone was excited and everyone was breathing a sigh of relief. Thirty minutes later, the loudspeaker would click again. By the time I punched out, we had closed to within twenty-five miles.

Amanda's parents were off at a fund-raiser or something, so it was up to us to accompany Oscar trick-or-treating. He was dressed up like a soldier in camouflage, a flak jacket, a plastic helmet, and a plastic bazooka. Since it was cold, he had to wear a coat and hat and scarf, so the only thing that made him look like a soldier was the bazooka. He didn't seem to care. He wasn't such a bad kid.

It was such a long walk between each big house that it took a while for us to get from one destination to the next. In the dark, you could hear people calling "trick or treat," but you couldn't see them, you could only see glowing pumpkins. Oscar held Amanda's hand, and Amanda held my hand, and I imagined that this was what it might be like for me, twenty years in the future, walking with Amanda through some rich neighborhood on Halloween with our son or daughter. She probably wouldn't marry me, though. She'd marry one of those successful guys with a college degree and a normal body. That was most likely what the future held in store for me, I thought.

"Bang bang!" Oscar said when the doors opened. In reply, the homeowners gave him generous handfuls of candy, which he didn't mind sharing with Amanda and me.

At one point along the way, we stopped in the road to say hi to some of his little buddies from school. They stared at my empty sleeve and said, "What happened to your arm, mister?"

"It's congenital," I said.

"What's that mean, mister?"

"It means it got shot off in the war."

They liked this.

By the end of the night, we had ten pounds of candy.

"Can I stay up?" Oscar said when we got home. He wanted to count everything. He had chocolate all over his mouth.

"No," Amanda told him. Then they screamed at each other. Then he went to bed. Then it was just the two of us.

It was quiet except for the ticking of the grandfather clock coming from somewhere deep within the house. We sat on the couch together. My good arm around her shoulder, her leg pressing against my leg.

I said, "This is what it could be like for us."

"What could be like for us?" she said.

"You and me in this house."

"We are in this house," she said. She didn't get it.

"You don't get it," I said.

She unwrapped one of her brother's lollipops and stuck it in her mouth. She watched me watch her. She leaned over and put her lips close to my ear. I could smell the strawberry. "Come on," she whispered, "let's go upstairs." Her breath made my toes curl. "I have to work in the morning" was all I could think to say. It was true. But I followed her up the big staircase anyway, tiptoeing past Oscar's room, and then across the landing, and then up another staircase that led to her bedroom.

It was small and cozy, with slanted ceilings, and it was decorated with the pinks and purples of her childhood. She had fluffy pillows all over the bed. She had posters of kitty cats on the wall. Sitting on her dresser were a hundred tiny bottles and jars. On cue, she opened a tube and squeezed a small amount of cream on her finger. She rubbed it into her cheeks and forehead.

"One of these days," she said, "I'm going to wake up in the morning and be cured."

"If you believe it," I said, "it will happen." I was quoting. She looked in the mirror at me. "Is that so?"

"Good things happen to good people," I said.

She snickered. "Who told you that?"

I couldn't remember.

Abruptly, she asked, "Do you think I'm pretty, Max?"

"I sure do," I said. Because I did. And to show my sincerity, my romantic interest, I put my good arm around her waist and kissed the back of her neck. But she'd had enough with kissing. She whirled around and stuck her finger in my belt loop and pulled me against her. She was surprisingly strong and her breasts were pressed against my chest. She tugged at my shirt. I twisted awkwardly but she wouldn't let go.

"Can't we at least," I said, "turn off the light?"

"No," she said.

"Please," I pleaded.

Back and forth we went like this, me wiggling and squirming, she pulling and tugging, me the object of desire, she the kleptomaniac, until finally, too exhausted and embarrassed to go on, I succumbed.

"Okay, okay," I said.

She relaxed her hold on me at once. It felt like a snake uncoiling. Then she reclined with a sigh onto her purple bed, her back propped up by a dozen pillows, her hands behind her head in a posture of luxuriousness.

I stood there in the middle of her bedroom, the lights blazing away, as bright as those fluorescent lights in the supermarket, and I did what she wanted: I undressed. The shoes first, of course, then the socks, and after that I took off my belt because I was stalling for time, and then I unzipped my jeans and stepped out of them, and after that I dropped my boxers, since I'd rather be naked from the waist down than from the waist up. But soon there was nothing left except my shirt, which I unbuttoned as slowly as I could, until my chest was exposed with one sleeve hanging full and one sleeve hanging empty. Then I took it all the way off.

I stood there naked and silent, waiting for her to issue her verdict about my deformity, which presently she did: "What's the big fucking deal, Max?"

Then she turned off the lights and pulled me onto her bed, where she spent the next few hours teaching me how to do all those things I'd only ever watched in the videos.

In the morning I woke late. I was late for work. I didn't care. I lay there without moving, next to Amanda in her fluffy bed. Then very quietly I got up and got dressed and sneaked downstairs past her parents' bedroom, where I could hear a white noise machine whirring, and out the back door.

In the daylight, the Halloween displays had lost their power to frighten; they were flat and wilted and wet. During the night the ghosts and goblins had fallen or been torn down, and now the roads were covered with pillowcases and cardboard, pounded into the ground by a succession of cars, mine included. The American flags were flying, though, they were flapping in the wind, and when I came over the river, the factories were going strong.

Everyone said that it was only a matter of time until we took the capital, maybe a matter of hours. But every time the loudspeaker clicked on that day, it was just Mr. Moskowitz letting me know that there was a cleanup in such-and-such aisle, and I would wheel my mop and bucket the other way.

For two days people walked around holding their breath,

looking expectantly at one another. For two days everyone waited to hear what would happen next.

And on the third day the draft began.

Pink from coffee was called right away. So was Howie from deli. So were three baggers and someone from fish and someone from bakery. Ziggy was called. He'd gotten his wish after all.

You could tell who was going by the way he walked, slowly, deliberately, as if groping his way through a rainy night. If I happened to make eye contact with one of them, they would look startled. I tried to avoid them when I could. Within a week they had gotten their papers, and they had gotten their physicals, and the day before they were to depart, we had a surprise going-away party for them. Everyone gathered in the back room, including some customers who'd been shopping in the supermarket for years and knew everyone by name. When the recruits arrived, they pushed their way through the swinging doors, and we shouted, "SURPRISE!" But the surprise was on us, because they'd gotten their heads shaved and they looked strange, like newborns. I couldn't even recognize them. The baggers looked like they'd give anything to go back to bagging.

"You boys look so handsome," one of the cashiers said. The men tried to smile, but they knew the truth. They stood with their arms folded meekly in front of their chests.

Mr. Moskowitz said, "Eat up, everyone!" And we ate our free doughnuts and drank our free sodas that Mr. Moskowitz had gotten the district manager to donate. No one really knew what to say. We tried to mill around, but it was difficult because the back room was cramped with the day's delivery, the pallets stacked one on top of another, ten high, towering over our heads. It was a reminder that all of these boxes would soon be opened and unpacked, so as to make room for the next day's delivery—life goes on.

Eventually Mr. Moskowitz said he wanted to make a speech. Everyone got quiet and he stood on a box and started by saying how he was proud of each of the guys, even though they didn't have any choice in the matter.

"What you're doing," he intoned, "what you're about to do . . ."

Ziggy and Howie stared straight ahead—they already had the stare of soldiers. Pink had his eyes closed because he was high. The baggers stared at their feet.

"I know it's going to turn out all right for you," Mr. Moskowitz said, "because you're good people."

The room said yes to that.

"You're going to be back soon," he said.

The room said yes to that too.

"It's not easy," Mr. Moskowitz said, "but it's important." His voice was rising, and his face was getting red, and some of the cashiers were wiping their eyes, and the mood was becoming even more doleful and downcast, and the back room was hot, unbearably hot, and I had the feeling that we were at a funeral, not a going-away party, that this was it for Ziggy and Pink and the baggers. They wouldn't be coming back. Their faces told the story.

So I shouted, "Shoot some motherfuckers for me, fellas!" And that broke the tension. The back room erupted, everyone applauded, including Pink and Ziggy and the guy who collected shopping carts in the parking lot. After that, we ate and

drank our fill and talked about other things until Mr. Moskowitz said it was time for us to get back to work.

Later that day, as I was coming out of the locker room, Mr.
Moskowitz called me into his office. "Max," he said. He
sounded exhausted. "Come in, Max, and shut the door." The
knot in his tie was loose because it was the end of the day, it
was casual time. He put his hands on his spreadsheets and
looked at me from across the desk, a paternal, patient look. A
look of forbearance.

What wrong thing, I wondered, had I done now.

"If you give one hundred percent, Max," he said, "you get
one hundred percent right back."

And the next morning at nine o'clock sharp, I changed into
my new uniform and took my place behind the coffee bar. I
had been right, it's not hard to pour a cup of coffee, especially
when you have a five-dollar raise to go along with it.

That winter I learned fast and I learned well, and the customers would come walking up to the counter, tracking slush
across the floor, which was no longer my problem, and I'd
make their mochas and their cappuccinos and their lattes with
a smile and a flourish. Sometimes Amanda would stop in unannounced, sometimes with her parents—who were proud of
me—and little Oscar, who had started teaching me how to
snowboard, which I had a surprising proclivity for. I'd turn
around and they'd be standing there waiting for me to notice
them. Amanda would be wearing that old fur coat with the
American-flag pin.

"May I help you?" I'd ask, as if they were customers whom
I'd never seen before. It was a game we played, and it never

failed to get a laugh. Then I'd make their drinks how I knew they liked them—hot chocolate for Oscar.

When they were done drinking and chatting, Mom and Dad would say that they should let me get back to work. They'd wave goodbye. "So long! So long!" Amanda would stay a few moments longer, leaning across the counter to kiss me on the lips, and with that expert sleight of hand she had mastered somewhere long ago, she would slip a single packet of sugar into her coat pocket.

Acknowledgments

I am indebted to my agent, Zoë Pagnamenta, and to my editors at the Dial Press, Noah Eaker and Susan Kamil.

Many thanks also to Cressida Leyshon, Deborah Treisman, David Remnick, Philip Gourevitch, Nathaniel Rich, Matt Weiland, Jean Strouse, Kelle Ruden, Joanna Yas, Jessica Flynn, Sarah Levitt, Caitlin McKenna, Dani Shapiro, Michael Maren, Sharmila Woollam, Caroline Dawnay, Bryan Charles, Laurie Sandell, Keith Josef Adkins, and Thomas Beller. As well as to the Whiting Foundation, the Cullman Center for Scholars and Writers at the New York Public Library, the New York Foundation for the Arts, New York University, and Housing Works Bookstore Café (where several of these stories were written).

And every Wednesday evening at 6:45, Jeff Adler, Andrew Fishman, and Jeff Golick.

ABOUT THE AUTHOR

SAÏD SAYRAFIEZADEH was born in Brooklyn and raised in Pittsburgh. He is the author of *Brief Encounters with the Enemy* and a memoir, *When Skateboards Will Be Free*. His writing has appeared in *The New Yorker*, *The Paris Review*, *Granta*, *McSweeney's*, *The New York Times Magazine*, and *The Best American Nonrequired Reading*, among other publications. He is the recipient of a Whiting Writers' Award and a fellowship from the Cullman Center for Scholars and Writers. He lives in New York City with his wife and teaches at New York University.

ABOUT THE TYPE

This book was set in Sabon, a typeface designed by the well-known German typographer Jan Tschichold (1902–74). Sabon's design is based upon the original letter forms of Claude Garamond and was created specifically to be used for three sources: foundry type for hand composition, Linotype, and Monotype. Tschichold named his typeface for the famous Frankfurt typefounder Jacques Sabon, who died in 1580.